Christmas 1982.

Yer
Last
Decadent

Charlie Farquharson

Yer Last Decadent

Don Harron

Macmillan of Canada
A Division of Gage Publishing Limited
Toronto, Canada

CANADIAN CATALOGUING IN PUBLICATION DATA

Harron, Don, date
    Charlie Farquharson, yer last decadent

ISBN 0-7715-9722-3

1. Canada—History, Comic, satirical, etc. I. Title.

FC173.H37   971.064′4′0207   C82-094724-5
F1026.4.H37

Design: Franklin Hammond

All photographs courtesy of Canapress Photo Service reproduced with permission.

Macmillan of Canada
A Division of Gage Publishing Limited

Printed in the United States of America

Fer Calf Run
Mick Kinnon
(the wife's
faverit singer)

Con Tents

Inner Duckshun

Ten yeer ago I rit a histry of Canda that coverd the ground frum the cremation of yer Universal up till the summer of 1972. (It tuck 128 pages fer to tell all that.) I allus rite books wen I can't git out on the land to plow. This winter wuz so blaim bad I didden even git my rocks off till laid in May. So instead I rit a histry of Canda frum wher I left off before. It cuvvers from September 1972 till yer Spring of '82, yer fall of one decadent to the deekline of anuther. The mazin thing is that it tuck 128 pages fer to tell all this, too. I don't know wether it was on accounta inflayshun, or the fack that the last ten yeers has bin jist as fulla happnins as the last two or three billyun put together. You'll just have to be the jedge fer yerself. Myself, I'm gittin back on the land for the harrowing days ahed.

Yers sin seerly
Charles Ewart Farquharson
Ornery Sittizen
Yer Last Decadent

Chapter 1.   1972

The Big Inning of Yer Fall

It's all ways darkist before it dawns on yuh. Let's hope that old sayin' is true after the decayed we jist bin thru. Most of what has happen in the last ten yeer is bad, I grunt yuh, but looking back in wreckrowspeck, yer fall of '72 don't seem to be that much of a downer. In fack, it started out with one of our biggest uppers we have had sints that liddle French mare, Jeans Dropout, had his big Expose in '67.

You'll mind '72 was the yeer we started up yer World's Serious of Hockey with them Serviette Roosians. Oh, we'd clashed with them before, incloodin' the time where we won with yer Smokey Tail Eaters, a Rocky hockey teem frum Birdish Clumberya. But them fellers was part of yer Canajun Hammerchewer Hockeyists, so they give 'em all a Climax watch and fergot about 'em. Well sir, if they was unperfessional so is them Roosians still, and if you look at the statisticleticks since '54, they still mange to beet our NH Hellers at ther own game. We have played agin yer Red 410 times since '54, and they has beat us a lot morn we bit them: 282 to 96 with 32 tie.

Mind you, hockey ain't Canda's nashnulistic sport. It's La Crotch, a old Injun game plaid with warp tennis rackits. Besides, our hockey was export to the States when we was in our sixties and it got so expansive they went frum six team to twelve. That's when the game stop bein' smooth round yer edges and got ruff in yer corners. They started settin' out a goon to stop a goal. Soon's our boys come out on the ice they'd be checkin' their boddys, slappin' their shots, mixin' it up and heddin' fer yer peanulty box. Never mind skatin' or passin' or enny of that kinda foreplay.

Talk about yer Cold War, we was reddy fer to do battle with them Roosians. And fer them of us as was simble-minded it shape up like Wirld War Three, which has so far bin kep on ice.

Yer Inner Nashnul Seen

Mind you, back in '72, ther was a reelive hot war goin' on over there to Veet Napam. And even in Yerp things was heetin' up. Yassir Arrowfat and his Pale Stine Terrierassts sure rooned yer Mewnick Olimprix, and started sending thru the males their litter bums. And sum rich Germin kids called yer Badoff Minors ganged up agin ther eldern and got reely revolting when they started adultnapping big biznessmen. In lttly peeple started gittin' ther knees capped by yer Red Brig Aids, who capped it all off a yeer later when they hijack ther own Premeer that was, till he wernt no more.

Lotsa planes got hijack that yeer. We oney had one of them in Canda, musta bin the oney happy hi-jackin in history. This plane tuck off frum Dubblin hedded fer Newyork, when sumbuddy on board went upfront and stuck a Mouser in yer Pile-it's eer, and order him to gofer Havanner, Cuba. Seems there wern't enuff gas fer all that, and this IRAte jacker, or Shinny Faner, or dopeydeeler, whatever he wuz, dint want the plane to refool on Yank soil, so it hedded fer Trontuh. When the Yanks herd about it, they tole ther lokel C.I.A. fella to take off his R.C.M.P. unyform and put on his F.I.B. badge, and git out to yer Malted Airport. Yer hijacker musta got his wind up about this fer when that plane touch down at yer Interminable Number One it dun it oney on one weel, then tuck off agin up yer wild blewyonder with a few F.I.B. shots whistlin' at ther tires. The happy part about the hole thing is that the plane finely made it to Havanner, and it work out so good, they now have the regler service with Ireland, yer CubaLingus.

Back to Yer athaleet's Feets

But I'm gittin' side-track by this high jack-off. The main eevent of '72 was yer Canda's Cups wich start off erly in Septmber in yer Make Beleeve Gardings, and that first

9

game turn out to be a freeassco fer our side.

Oh, our boys begun pritty good. After the first few mints of yer first peeriod she was 2 nuthing fer us before you could of sed Ripsky Korsetsoff, Shakeroffsky or Shostakovitchsmallbyerwaterfall. It look like Roosians was pritty good decomposers of classified musick but as hocky plairs they was well on ther way to Oblivia. They all looked unanimuss anyways, you codden tell hoo's hoo under all them crashed helmitts.

Foster Hooey kep callin' out ther names frum up his gundoler, and he sounded like he was comin' down with the hay feever. Yaketyshev!! Maltsoff! Anacin!! Harmthemall!!!! But by yer third peeriod them Redskates was walletzin' rings round our fellas to the tune of 7-3.

There was a lotta openmouths in the Trawntuh Urena that nite, and a coupla booze fer Teem Canda.

When them Roosians left Canda they was leedin' our teem two game to one, and cooden wait to git at it agin in Mawscow. They almost got fool in that first game on Serviett soil when it looked like ourn fer sure. We was four to one till the last six minits when we let them bang in four goal regler as crockwork.

That ment our boys hadda win the next three strait, but them Muskyvites didden know we had a seecret wepping. We didden neether. His name was Pall Hendyson, and he tide up yer Serious fer us in the next two game.

Cum yer last game, yer tie-broker, and them Cockasians was leedin' us goin into yer thurd peeriod, 5-3. Then by gollies, we cum alongside neckineck, 5-5. What happen then was a kind of mirrorcull, and I think pert neer all 22 millyun Canajuns was watchin' when Polly Hendyson flu thru the air and pit it in with 34 seckins to go.

We had reeched our gole. It was like a nashnul dream writ by that P.R. Berton. And as Winsome Churchle used to say, it was our Finesse Tower.

Gamey Pollyticks

But in that bigger game outside the rink, it were less of a fairy's tail. We lost a cuppla good ones in '72, Lister Bee

Who kneed Terdo?

Piercin and Hairy Trueman, and we sure coulda dun with
both of them. The one fer to keep actin' as peeskeeper in
yer MidLeast, and the tother to stick around yer White
House and give a little Hell to yer present encumbrance,
Tricky Nixon.

That was the yeer Dirty Dicky got re-selected pert neer by axlimation over the Demmycrap Sentaur McGubbern. Mind you, she was a pritty low turnup of voter out to axercise ther frenchfrise, but Big Dick give everybuddy two fingers up, and act like he was to be coryonated over to Westminis Dear Abby. But I spose his topper fer '72 was havin' tee in reel China cups with Mousey Tung. This had bin all deranged fer him the yeer before by his Stately Seckaterry, Henry Kissassinger, who spent a lotta time opening them Peeking doors fer him. Us Canajuns had bin havin relations with Peekinese fer quite some time, but nobuddy paid much mind to it.

We had a lection of our own that yeer, and nobuddy paid much mind to that neether. Leest of all Premiere Terdo, who had been give a big Man Date in '68 when he tuck off his close and dun a backflip offa his divin' bored, and then all our wimmen went strait to their ballet boxes and dun the same fer him. I ast the wife and former sweetheart why she was votin' fer him. "On accounta his blue eyes and his brown belt." That belt was frum doin' the Judy-o. I told Valeda: "I got me a brown belt, too. It holds my pants up, but that don't mean it's gonna do the same fer the hole country."

But that first time by gittin' down to his skin he was in like Flin Flon with them Terdomaniacs. He went around in his helluvacropper shoutin': "I kin promiss you nothing! Nothing! Nothing!" And in the next four yeer he seceeded in livin' up to every promiss.

But he still seem to be the darlin' of Jest Society peeple. And most of us thot he'd breeze thru to the next four yeer without even fuddling his duddle. He never bother to peer at enny Libreeal fund-razor ralleys, wich would pay fer his lectoral shampane. He more or less foned in his speaches. Sed he peefurred talkin' direct to peeple without other pollytishuns or their issue gittin' in the way.

His slowgun was "Lalond Is Strong". My boy Orville thinks I'm wrong, but that's nuthin' new. He thinks it was "The Land Is Strong" but I don't think even them Grits woulda had the nerve fer to say that. The oney time the land is strong round about my parts is durin' spreddin' time.

His mane proponent was yer Leeder of yer Opposite Position, Regressive Preservative Bob Stansfeeld, who had sed farewell to Novas Kosher as a pervincial premeer and was tryna slide into Ottawa on banana appeel. He had riz up thru the trap door of his famly's undyware bizness in Truerow, and was now tryna unseat Truedow. He pert neer dun it. When the votes was all count up that nite it look like a toss-off eether way, haff a dozen of one and sexpack of the tother. Neckineck all nite, them two leeders was closer'n the cheeks of a Clidesdale's arse in fly-time.

Finely nex morning, Pee Air had got in by the skin of one or two of his private member. And when he give a pressed confidence, a lotta peeple thot he mite rezine fer

Two Big Drips

to stay home with his bewdyfull bride, Mar Grit. She look like she was in shock treetmint fer an eclectic fit that nite. But her husbin jist put on his enematic smile and told his country that weather it was clear to them or not, his Universal was folding up, as it should.

And after that Sinderella gole in Mawskow, I spose everybuddy figgered he must be rite. God and Pee Air was both on our side, what more did we want? But Premire Terdo is a skeer, not a hocky plair, and ever since yer fall of '72 it's bin all downhill for him and us too.

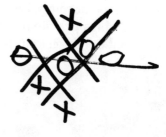

Chapter 2.   1973

The Rising of Yer O Pecker

Sebbenty-three waz one of yer turn-in points of histry.
All our trubbles seem to cum frum yer Mid-Least, and I
don't mean New Brunsick: them poor fiddlerheds never
dun nobuddy no harm. I'm talkin' about yer Arb dessert
where all the sheek peeples lives. Durin' 1973 they quadra-
poopled ther oily prices frum two bucks a barl up to ate.
Yessir, them fellahs in the harem-scarem pants and the
slippers with the pointy toes finely put the boots to us, and
they've kep us over a barl ever since.

I never noo we had a ellergy crysis till that yeer. When
I was a little tad back in yer twennies, oil never seem so
all-fire important. I think our famly maid it thru the hole of
a summer on jist ajar of Vassaleen. Most of it went fer yer
binder and thrasher, and the rest went fer Sex: Ma and Pa
used to put it on the outside nob of ther bedroom door so's
us kids cooden git in the room.

In them days our oil 'n grease cum lokel frum a place
called Peter Rollyuh, hard by Sarnyuh, Ont. We din't have
to go over to our Yank naber and borry a cup; in them
days we was wat they call nowaday self-defishunt.

But buy and buy, I bleeve it was yer old Rocky Feller
hoo got us hook on the stuff. Johnny Dee Rockyfeller (that
was) set the Standerd fer Oil by buying up all of his oppo-
sitposition. That's how he got us by the juggler vane with
his import greasy skid stuff. Did jever see a pitcher of the
old skinny flint? I dunno wat good all that munny dun him.
It sure didden make the old tyfoon ever look happy. Had a
spression on his face like he was always squeezin' the life
outa a dime.

Anuther reeson fer this oil shortedge was becuz we
had all gone plastick jist after World War Too. Oil was use
fer everything, incloodin' them pink flamin' goze on all yer

lawns of yer sluberbs. But it wernt till this here yeer, 1973, that them Arbs start cuttin' us off by puttin' a turnkey round our necks. They called it an unbargo.

Sum peeple say it was yer Yung Nipper War with Izzreel that was yer straw that put yer camel on its back. That war look to me like anuther summer rerun of yer 1967 freeasco. So yer Panned Arb Fedreeation — yer Shoddy Arabian, yer Abby Dabbyers, yer Jordan Inanians, yer Syriac, and yer Libberer — all rared up and put the cap on our oil.

But trooth to tell, this oily ratfite reely start to sizzel back in yer fiftease. We din't know it at the time, but it was all cause by a fella name of Munro Bathbun who worked as a zeccativ fer Golf. Wen I say Golf I don't mean yer clubbin' ballgame. I meen that malted nashnul oily cumpny tuck over all our B.N.A. gastations back in '67. They musta noan that Premeer Terdo was gonna cancel yer B.N.A. and start a act of his own that wuz more constitootional. But yer Golf act that cause all the trubble by 1973 was this fella Bathbun decidin' all by hisself that them Arbs was gittin' too much munny fer ther oil. I dunno wat they was skimmin' offa the top but we was oney payin' two bucks yer barl fer our retail. And this Bathbun fella, with more nerve than a stop-up canal horse, cut back on them Arb prophets. As far as I'm concern, it was him thunk up the mess we are in today, and his name shud go down in histry as fur as it kin go, along with Eadie Allmean, Gangreen Kan and Atiller yer Hun.

It sure seem a cawshun that a buncha old fossils who all decade about 250 millyun yeer ago got as high in this decayed as fourty dollar a barl. Yer Opecker sheek claim they hadda riz ther rates on accounta the high cost of livin' it up brung about by Western inflayshun. I woodna thot they wood be so afflickted by what happens in our Prayery provinces.

Mind you, Elberta with the help of yer Arb sure went thru the changes after 1973. They had been no grate sheiks — except old blooeyes hisself, Luffhed — until them Arbs started to sit on ther oily depossits. That unbargo brot a

16

yelp of pane from Yerp to Japanned, but all it brot from Elberta wuz a big Tarsands yell, and the boom wuz herd all over the West. For the rest of us it has spelt trubble ever sints. Persnally, I don't thinks it's so bad fer yer urbane peeple, cuz they've got ther rabbit transits, slubways, GoGo trains and yer Dial-a-Prare busses. Accorn to statis-tickleticks, yer avridge sitty driver is in his car mebby four hour a day, but he goes lessen five mile. No reeson why most of them cooden become streetwalkers.

Canada's navel power gets the wind up on yer energy shortedge

Pollyticks

But what wuz Ottawar doin' about all this? Yer Grits in the Common House wuz over ther own barl. They wuz oney two seets ahed of yer Tory, and jist hangin' in by the skinny-skin-skin on yer End D.P. Terdo had lern a lessen from that leckshun of 72, wich left him and Stansfeeled closer than the uncut pages of *Hanserd*. He reelized to stay in power he hadda be cum less of yer fillossifer King and more of yer Mick Kenzy King. That's why he decide to shack up with Daisy Loose, the Socialite leeder hoo maid fun of both Terdo's and Stansfeeled's corpulent well-fed bums. So Terdo tole his Cabnut that to make up fer this shortedge of oil, he wuz goin' have to have a coalishun under the table, playin' footsy with yer Leftys.

Energy cutbacks was eezy fer them shrivel servants: they bin in practiss fer yeers. The Minister without the Energy fer to Mind Our Resources, Ronald Macdonald, tole the rest of us to cut back too, by ternin' the lites out and goin' to bed more erly. This brung about the danger of a copulation exploshun. Sure nuff, nine months later to the day, Pee Air and Daisy Loose gave berth to Peter O'Can, the guvmint's own tar baby.

Three munths later Pee Air gave berth agin. Ackshully, it was Mar Grit dun it but he got the assist. Little Justin Time wuz born Deesember 25, and sum peeples thot it were a mirrorcull. But if you count back nine munth you gits to April 25. Now bout that time there's plenny a huzbins walkin' the floor over ther incum tax, not knowin' what to do. But Pee Air know what to do: he got hisself anuther big deduckshun jist afore the yeer was out!

Turn Relay Shuns

Ther was still that unoffishull war goin' on over to Veet Napam, but us Canajuns was all sposed to be nooter and out of it, apart from all the armymints we sold.

Canda becum part of a peeskeeping farce sent over to Sigh-gone by yer Unightied Notions fer to overlook yer

18

hostility. We was sposed to bring bout a seezing of yer fire so's both sides cood get a little piece. They was three parts to yer teem: us, yer Pole and yer Injun. I don't meen the kinda Injun yer guvmint has the reservations about; I meen the ones that ware a dyper around ther hed like they're well-hung over. I dunno wat yer Pole wore, but our fellas stood out from the lot in ther darkygreen Yewnickfication soots. They musta bin itchin' to ware ther shorts in that topical climax, but I bet it bug them a bit, speshully when ther's so much room for the creepys to crawl up.

1973 was the yeer they finely got yer seizefire after three yeer of drinkin' tee over to Paris France hard by yer Iffy Tower, between yer Ewe Ass Stately Seckaterry Hennery Kissassinger, and that Hannoyd gorilla with the web feet, Le Duck Toes. They used to fite over not only hoo was gonna pay the bill, but neether of them like the shape of the table they were squabblin' on. I think them fellas had it too soft, argyin' all day, and goin' off by nite to yer Fal-lease Brazeers fer to watch the girls can cans.

I tell yuh, if they'd of set them two dimpledmats on toppa my manoor pile in Parry Sound, they wooda rap the hole thing up in one hot day. I think the biggest sprize of all that yeer was Kissassinger gittin' yer Nobel Peesprize. Nobel, that's oney five mile frum Parry Sound. Mind you, he never got so much as a honnerbull menshun frum us.

Utter Space

If I din't know what on Erth yer Yank was doin', I was even more confuse by yer spaced-out pogrom that yeer. First of all, there was a lotta talk about a comet call Koho-tex. I dunno why it had all the pastronomys jumpin up and down, fer it was gonna miss us by a millyun mile.

But the big thing that year that got off the ground frum yer Emishuns Control at Cape Carnivoral was yer Skyflab. This was the Dumbo jet of all them little satellyites. You'll mind the Roosians were the first to do it with a dog, in one of them Spooknuts. They tot it to raze its laig every time it passover Norsamerka.

But yer Skyflab was biggern all them extrytestial objecks put together, bout the size of a condom-minimum apartmint. Like them others, it was bilt fer to circumsize the Erth every cuppla hours, but nobody seem to know what fer. The wife she figgerd the Yanks dun it fer to look down on us erthly morls, and mebby keep tab on all them drafty dodgers we was harborin' in Canda.

Whatever it was doin', I was kinda glad it was orebittin' beyond yer 200-mile limit where yer Law of Gravelty has never bin past. And it sure tuck the sails outa a lotta peeple had bin seein' UFO's that yeer. They clame these Unindemnifiable Far-out Objecks cum frum constelluhpations behind our Spiro's Nebulous. Now that Skyflab was up there, I cood tell these nuts that them flying sorcerers they seen was reely this big Yank Spooknut. But one feller cuppla consessions over from us clame he seen one land, and a cuppla unerthly creechers with antenemas on ther fourheds was walkin' around like landed immigrance.

Terned out they wasn't Marxians at all, but a coupla Rotarians hedded fer a Hollow Eeny party. Mind you, I'm not a compleet septic. It don't meen I don't bleeve ther ain't no extry planetarium travlers out there. I jist think them unerthlings is to smart to land. Oney reesin they hang around our solo sistern is to keep an eye on us wen we're gittin' our rockets off. They probly seen us sending up that big Skyflab, and was releefed to see we wasn't gittin' above ourselves like we used to. Fer the one thing them utter spacemen don't want is us emmygratin' over to the hemmysfeeroids in their galexlaxy. If we try movin' into their planterry naberhood, I betcha they'll be the ones yellin' at us: "Why don't UFO!"

I'm labor

arseselfs

We pert near struck out fer ~~ourselves~~ this summer of '73. We had stareo ferrystrikes goin' at both ends of us, both yer Atlantical P.E. Eyelanders and to be Spacific, yer Bee Seers too. Them boats stopped runnin' frum Uclueless to Cape Turpentine, and by the time it was over, neether provinshuls bleeved enny more in ferries.

And even tho' they was a continence apart, Premeers Dave Bart and Alex Camel was beside therselves. Dave, yer Endy Pier, musta wisht them Sociable Credit Cards was back in, so's he cood blaim his Laber panes on them.

Soon after yer fairys bump and grind to a halt, we went off yer rails as well. This made Libral Premeer Alex-camel maddern a wet hen. When the maneland was cut off, tooriests was pile up six to yer brest at Boredom, Pee Ee Eye, and Cap Turpentine, and your CNR wooden cum across. I tell yuh, them Marmtiders had more strikes agin them than a Bloojay that summer. After yer fairy and yer railer, out went yer bilders on a wildcatinhouse strike. Then yer mettle workers got together and decide not to give a sheet. And then, by swinjer, didden yer Hellfacts nurses go out and the streets was fulla them panhandlers. If yer plummers had pulled the plug like they thretten to, it wooda bin down the drane and farewell No Skoasher.

Other strikes happen in 1973, too, but it all seem to pail by comparson. Hamilton had a garbitch strike fer nine weeks and ther hole mountin looked so green all spring with all them Gladbags all over it. Undytakers was out too, and it was after Eester before they burried a livin' sole. The post-offiss strike never happen that yeer, on accounta they sent out the strike call by male, and nobuddy got it in time.

Not everybuddy was strikin' in '73. A horse by name of Sexyrotariat fullfill a childhood dreem of mine when he retire at the age of six to be a full-time stud. Turn out not to be as much fun as ya'd think. A lot of that horseplay is dun male order by artifishul insinuation. Seems a shame to bottle up a good draft horse.

Roilty and Precedents

Our Queen cum out fer a visit, at a time when we was cuttin' the Royls off of things. There was sum talk about changin' Royl Queen Bee Jelly to jist plane Jellycanda. And there was more snubversive talk about weather the Queen was worth her high celery, and if she ruled to work or jist worked to rule. And there was a lotta sneaky cricketsism about Prints Fill and sister Margrose and her hus-bin-that-was, Tony Strongarm Jones. But if you've watched them Royls takin' a tramp across the Moores with the porgies you'd reelize they is jis farm peeple like us, oney in their case a man's home *is* his cassel.

Better them lardships than wat them Yanks had to pitup with this yeer. Their present encumbrance, Richer Nixon, give the Good Housebrakin' Steal of Approoval to them Watery-Gate Found-ins, but he wern't yet found out.

Everybuddy sed best thing he dun in '73 was to fly over China and reccanize all them Peekinese. I gotta admit thass a good trick on accounta there's sposed to be neer a billyun of 'em.

One not-so-good trick was tryna sell off his ole loveletters to yer Lieberry of Congers. He was needy wen it cum to munny, he sed, and hadda lotta expanse fixin' up his two unwhitehouse places, Sam Quentin on yer Westcoast, and Keep Biscayin' in Florider nex to his lil pal, Baby Bozo.

His cheef vice was Spoorious Agnes and he got into sum kinda chickeninnery too. Sum kinda fiscal contortion over Mary'sLand when he was goobernar. Big Spoor, he figgerd his White Houseboss wood git the heet offa him, but Tricky Nixy seem to cum down with a staff infeckshun. Sum peeple sed he was suffern frum a live tapewurm. Nickson was so took with his own voice he used to reecord everything fur posteerior, even kep a portabull reseevin' set under his bed. So do we, but ars is bone chiner.

Leckshuns

It was a off yeer. Oney big exercise of frenchfrise was in Cuebeck where Robair Booracic beet the socks offen Reemy Leveckyou. The score was 102-8. Pee Air never help Booracic, after Robair veetoed him the yeer before in Vicktoria, wen Terdo tried to git all them pervinshul premeers to take his constitootional. Pee Air spent his time during the Cuebec shampane skinnydipping in the Berdish Houndyerass, and dancin' over to Mosscow with all them Red Squares.

Booracic won over yer Separators by showin' that he

cood give one sweet dam. This was yer Shamesbay Projeck and it was call that becuz he never once kinsult yer Injian about their abridge-in-all rites. But they had lern a lesson frum their Alasker Bruthers up the sloop, and they hire therselves a smart Muntry All lawyer fer to settle Booracic in his hash. As that lady Joyce Kildeer sed, "I think that mebby I shall never see, A white man smarter than a Cree."

Kissassinger sneeks a little peece

Spurts

The big spurts event of the yeer was bringin' bullfites to Canda. They tried this first in Linseed, Ontaryo, but the Human Sassiety wooden let them in, tole the Maxycan permoter to stick it somewhereselts.

It finely end up in Muntry All. They got yer lokel Cuebec bull, but they hadda import them Maxican jumpin yuman beans fer to gode the bull with their big toothpicks: what they call yer peckadildoes. They was there jist to teaze yer unhappy hoofer sumthin' feerce before they let in yer matted door. He's the one in the tite pants, lite soot, and Mickey Mouse hat. His job is to git two eers and a peece a tail frum that horny beest without skrewering hisself.

The big thing in this hole rang-dang-doo is yer momint of trooth. That's wen the bullfitter gits down on one knee with his reer end to that snortin' quiverin' pawin' mess of primestake. My gol, if I had bin like that, jist askin' fer it up the backside, my momint of trooth wood have come wen I hi-tail it over the fence. I kin take wat comes outa the bizness end of a bull, and spred it fur and wide, but I got no mind to be spred the same way, nosirreebillybob.

Mind you, I never herd of no bull gittin' ears and tailpeece offa a mattedoor. If one of them bullstickers gits in trubble, and looks like he's in fer a goring time, why them pickyerdoors jist rushes out with their peckadildoes fer to finish off the big beef by giving it the coope de grass.

But that ain't what went on in yer Urena in Muntryall in '73. This wernt no Maxycan fiasca, but a homegroan Canajun bullfite snoopervize by yer Human Sassiety under the Osspisses of yer Arse Peecey Ay. They give the bull shoulder pads and a big doremat on his back, so's that wen he got pin-cushied he never felt no thing. A dry bull-run. Mind you, 24 hour later he probly end up in a slotterhouse where he got kilt anyways, but without no expecterators shouting, "Oh, lay!"

That's the Canajun way: an outa site slotter in good taist. Like wen we joined Nate Toe, and them Yanks offer to lone us them Bowmark missy iles. But Longjohn Doofenbeeker didden want them to give him nukuler whorehed, so we end up with a atomical reactionary with blanks. We oney went haffway to Helen a handcar.

Chapter 3.   1974

Yer Yeer that Streeked by

This heer yeer started off with a big no-show and it
didden happen jist after Newyear's after we had all
banged our dishpans and blew our horn and broke our
rezzelutions. We was all tole to watch fer this commet
Kohotex. It was sposed to brush us with its tale on its way
to the sun, accorn to them asternuts on yer Skyflab who
kep takin' its pitcher.

Now yer sun is morn 90 millyun mile away. (And
bleeve me, there are a few mornins every winter when I
figger it's further away than that.) If this cumit hedded strait
into yer Solar's Plexus, it wood end up as a dirty wiff of
steem, but sum of them sears that fourtells the future
clamed there was a danged good chance it was gonna hit
us slam bang in the long etudes. So I cooden stop thinkin
bout this little hemmusfeeroid splittin' us up into partisip-
ples and bringin' everythin on yer Muther's Erth to a
fullstop. But as you kin now reelize, it never happen atall.
Blame thing miss us by a millyun mile, and probly disa-
peered up sumbuddy else's Black Hole.

Time got all mixed up in 1974. Yer Yank figgered they
cood save on ther litebills by goin' on yer Daylite Slavin
erly in Janyerry. Us stick-in-the-dork Canajuns stuck on yer
Standerd, but it didden make no nevermind to us farmers,
we works both ends of yer gravy-yard shift anyways. I
spose a person mite suffer if he lived in Winzer and
worked as a mugger in Deetroit. The Ewe Ass give up this
idea after jist one seeson, and ever since then has bin with
us in yer dark ages.

Spurts Cum Backs

Mohammy Alley, him as used to be jist common Cash
Clay til he went into yer Muslin, made a big cumback this

yeer. Yeer befour, Joe Frasy had druv him crazy by makin' him flop like a butterfly, sink like a bee, till he went flat on his own bumbull. But this yeer he went over to Afferker fer to fite Gorge Forman in Sighear, wich wuz yer new name foer yer Bulgin' Conga. Everbuddy thot that Alley wood find out that Forman is boss, but Gorge tern out to bee jist anuther canvasback. Alley clame that he was the last of the redhot Maumaus.

Teem Canda had anuther go at yer Servietts. This time we had sum biguns up front: yer Golden Jetser, Bob E. Hull, wearin' his new hedpeece parted on the side, and the grand ole young'un Gordeehow, hoo with his two sons, Mark and Trade, was playin down to Hewston where the three of them seemed to be the biggest peece of yer Asstros.

In that first game, the Roosians watched a man old enuff to be our prime minster elbowing his way thru them Redstars. Hull he was nockin' the barly outa the bin too with his slapped shots that razed the hare on everybuddy's hed but his own. The only hot flashes between them two seenyers was the sparks offa ther skates. But the only cups they cum back with frum Roosia was aloomingun ones between their laigs.

The craziest athaleet's feat this yeer belong to that stunted man, Evil Connival. He calls hisself the last of yer Roamin Radiators, same as them mercymarys menny centurions ago used to fite fer bred in the circuses at yer Collassulseemen. Evil Connival cum this yeer to yer Exhibishunist Park in Tronto, and trucked his Hardly Davidson over thirteen Big Macs. Later this same yeer he tried to do the same blame thing over yer Grand Cannon, but this time he muffed his dive. Can yawn

It wern't jist yer athaleets that wer into spurt this yeer. Participle-action wuz sumthing thunk up by yer guvmint fer sitty peeple to do wile we farmers was pullin' all the cows in the dark. Yer Departmint of Welth and Hellfire got intereseted in peeple's figgers wen they herd that a sixty-yeer-old Sweed cood beat the pants off of us at runnin' around in his undyware.

So peeple out in Saskytune, hoo was used to stayin' up haff the nite smokin' potash, suddinly started runnin' round ther blocks. They took after ther Governing General, Roly Itchener, hoo had bin doin' it round Riddylo Hall fer yeers. Premeer Terdo, hoo has allus bin a big athaletic supporter, kin touch his nees without bending the floor and stand on his hed fer five minits, lettin' the blud rush past his eye-browse. Then he jumps in his sidsidyized pool and rubs down with a good stiff towl till he feels Rosy all over. Valeda wunders if that brung on the later trubble with the Missus.

Torn a Fairs

The biggest eevent this yeer was close to home — jist across yer boarder at yer Watery Gates. There's been a lot under the bridgeworks sints this happen, but it seem to set a new standirt in politicul corrupshin. It start off as a little brake-in fer yer Publicans in '72, but tern out to be a big brake fer yer Demmycraps in '74. It end up with everbuddy sayin', "Nix on the precedent."

They's a lotta theerys about wat brung about Trick-sydicksy's dumfall, but I think it was his foolin' round with yer Eternal Revenyoo. You kin fool alla the peeple alla the time, sept them fellas. Now Nixon in '73, he oney paid bout a thousand dollars in tax, and he got away with that. But it oney made him more greedy. So he went down to his basemint and rap up all the papers he could find, both pubic and private — luvletters, butcherbills, any dam thing — and tried to sell them to the Liebury of Congers as a tax shelter fer his reclining yeers. If he'd of gotten away with it, everybuddy wooda follered soot. Watever you think of the man, wen it cum to payin' taxes he was a masterebator.

But they sure had him taped in yer Ovary Offiss, give or take 18 minits. He never expleet nun of his deletivs — nossir, no fuddlyduddlin' fer this big Dick. When his cohores got found out, he jist took evasive acting like slide-trips to Mawscow and Eejipt. He even tride to start World War 3 to take peeples' minds off his trubbles, but it didden work. After they thretten a subpenis on him, he seen the writin' on the Whitehouse wall and quit. So he end up impaired but not unpeached.

First thing Nixon dun wen he got back to San Clemency was fone his old home to talk to his sucksesser. Geritol Ford had bin anointed Vice in place of yer Speared Agnew. Eether yer Bellpeeple dint have very good conneckshuns or Trickydick didden speek up with his dulse tones. Watever Nixon was yappin' about, Ford cooden heer him too good, so morn once he ast his previous encumbrance to speak up. But Tricky never did, so finely Ford yelled "Pardon?" Nixon let out a woop and hung up. Trickydick's pardner had becum his pardoner. And in one fell woop, Ford had became a Edsel.

Nixon out of offiss

Things coodna bin much better over in yer Serviet Roosia, judgin' by the number of fokes clamberin' to steppe out. The most importunt defecator wuz a bookriter, Allsander Saltyvixen, hoo was write up there with Tallstory, Checkoff and Pastersnatch. Alex sure live up to his name when he get out too. Told us all off jist like he tole his feller Roosians; sed we wuz goin' to hell in our own handcar alongside of them Bullyshyviks.

28

The reeson he was let go over yer Urinal mountins was on accounta his book, *Goulash Archeryerbellygo*, wich ern a lotta roylty over our way. If ther's one thing them Commonests cant stand it's roylty, havin' decapassitated ther own wen they maid the Revulsion back in '17. So Saltyvixen end up in Swishyland, where they offer him asylum. You'd think he wooda put up with enuff funny bizness at home without endin' up on a foolish farm.

The tother defecator was a belly danser, McHail Richbitchneekoff. The wife got all of a tizzy albout this Bullshy danser with the swan legs. She was hopin' he'd settle and becum a naturaleyes Canajun, but like most of our highsteppers he went grand-jettin' off to yer States in sumthin called *Lay Siphileeds*. You'd wonder why they'd wanna do a dance about a sociable disease!

Worn Peece

The war of the yeer wuz held over to Sighpress, tween yer Terk and yer Geek. Our fellas was cot in the muddle as referees under yer Yew En Securatitty Blanket. We wuz sposed to be a bufferin state tween a buncha Turkeys in curled-up slippers and harem-scarem pants, and them Greasin' belly dansers with the palmpalms on ther toes and the tassholes on the hats. Sighpress used to be the bizness of yer Birdish Umpire but them was too bizzy in '74 makin' the Maltese cross.

Our guvmint musta bin drummin' up bizness fer the next war when they sold off sum of our atomical piles to Injure. We figgered, I spose, that they was goin' to use our radio-action fer to fite off fammin coz by splodin' copulayshun amung the Skindoos and yer Seeks and yer Muslins in Injure, what live by dyin' off like flys. I think we shooda kept on sendin' our markwiss weet insteda couple of meggatons of mushroom clowds. But the lady premeer, Injura Gandy, thot she would fill up the beggin' boles with nukuler fishin. The GoodBook sez that if you throw yer crusts upon the waters, they'll back up to you. I wunder if the same thing happens with our bags of hevvy water?

29

Pollyticks   Turnker

   This was another leckshin yeer. John Turnip presented
his budgie and a lotta peeple resented it, cloodin' yers
trooly. I dunno why his "sustanchel tax cuts" cum to about
three sense, wile his "sleight increese on yer taxabull
incum" hit me fer about two hunnert doller. Us small mixed
farmers was startin' to git squoze out by what they call yer
aggravabizness. This ment big soopymarkits like Dumb-
minion and Bobloblaw wuz cuttin out us muddlemen and
byin' us out direck. Them typhoons gits all the bissness and
we git all the aggra-vayshun.
   The Grits had bin hangin' in fer two yeer by the seet of
ther pants but they finely all fell out wen they upped us at
the pumps ten cents per gal. I'll say one thing fer yer hed of
Imperriousoil, W.O. Twits, he was honest enuff to admit he
was makin money out of yer so-call shortedge. If you ast
me, we was the twits. I tole Valeda not to bother havin' our
analversary poortraits took by one of them Polarhem-
moroid cameras on accounta we had alreddy bin dun in
oils.
   Most of yer leckshun shampane was all wet. In sixty
daze electionreering we had forty of rain. The speeches
started and I thot about takin out crap insurance. But everything bugged us farmers that yeer. Grasshoppers got the
jump on us in Saskatchewin, plus a hole messa catterpillers
underfoot, and the only catterdepillertories aloud by law
seem to give the bugs a poorfumed sitzbath wich seem to
refresh them so's they cood git on the go agin. When the
Army wurms cum in frum the sands at Camp Boredom it
was time to commit insecticide.
   The Opposite positions worked harder than yer Inpee-
ple. Bob Stansfeeled, Daisy Loose, and even Real Cowette
was runnin around the country like chickens with ther ali-
mony cut off. Premeer Terdo, first thing he dun was skip the
coop. Flue down to a U.S. Universalty fer to git anuther
honerbull degree. He awreddy had two: a lotta us wanted
him to stay home so's we cood give him the third degree.

30

The place he went to git it happen to be ex-resident Nixon's old almamammy. That was when we found out that Nixon never took too much to our Pee Air. Mebby he thot Terdo was the tool of a oil company, becuz he is sposed to have sed "Here comes that Asso." This idee musta spred, fer wen yer Japanee premiere Tanacker of Toke-yo visit Ottawa, first thing he said wen he see Pee Air was "Ah So!" You figger it out.

Deef rates Bob's lecshun chantses

Stansfeeled git a lotta his Retrogessiv Preservatives mad by cummin' out fer Pricy Wage Controls. Some peeple thot that his wantin' to put the freeze on things wuz jist so his famly cood sell a lot of undyware before Chrissmuss. He said that if the premeer wanted to stop the rot he shood freeze it fer 90 daze. Terdo aloud as how it cood stand up by itself. In the end yer score wuz Librals 141 to Tories 95. Yer New Demmycraps wuz way down frum before fer beddin' with yer Grits. Them Sociables lerned that they shooden be so frendly with ther class enemas frum now on.

Leest one good thing happen on yer politiccull seen this year, when we got our new Governing Generull. Seems the job of being yer Vice-Wriggle goes thru the changes every four years. The new fella wuz Jewel LeJay. Sounds like one of them Tronto baseballers, but his bruther was one of yer Cardinals, spent all his time in Afferka training lepperds.

I think we bin pritty lucky with our Geegees ever since we went lokel with Vince Messy. Mind you, we had sum blooribboners before him: Lord Bang, hoo give atrophy fer slappin' the most shots in honour of his wife, yer Lady Bang; Lord Stanley, hoo started us all in our cups; Lord Tweedsmanuir, who writ all them books you can still reed up at Read-o Hall in that speshul place bilt fer them, yer Buchan Wing; and the biggest catch of them all, Feeledmarshal Alexander of Tuna.

Fads 'n Scandles

Ther was a big dustup in Trawna over topfull waitresses and bottomless bellyrub parlers. They both seem to rub the law the rong way. I never met anybuddy bin in eether. Mebby its becuz our kinda peeple don't need that kinda stimmlation. The wife and I strips fourteen cows twice a day. We git all the massage and creem we need. I spose sitty fellers is depraved of all this.

Accorn to that feller with the funny ears used to be on the Star Dreck on the TV, Dr. Spock, if you never got spankt wen you was a tad, the oney way to work off yer gilt edges is to hire some perfessional masshoor fer to do it. Imagine payin' fer sich capitalist punishment!

As fer them bearbrest servingirls, mebby the udder fassination of it all makes up fer them ineddible oils they puts in yer coffee. If peeple is razed on bottles insteada draft before they is weened, no wunder life seems to them a compleet bust.

Anuther downer this yeer was the strenth of our beer. Down frum 4 point 4 to 3 present. And they also tride to diloot our beer advertizemints. Marg Lalonde didden want all them Molten Golden Girls winkin' and laffin' and joo-kin' and lookin' up at a big bloo bloon wile they guzzled down suds. I think he wooda peefurred sum old rubbydub-dubs lyin' in a alley thrown up in our face. But it never hap-pen. Mebby the broors sent the bill for ther ads to them Alkyholicks Unanimous.

The biggest scandle was a new hobby called streekin.' It started zippin by in March and it kep peeples mouths open till fly-time. Lotsa peeple had bin streekin' fer yeers indoors, mostly tween the bedroom and the bathroom. The wife duz this every time she sees anuther gray hare, and runs and grabs her Greasin Formuler.

But this new kinda streekin' made peeples hare stand on end, fer this was runnin' about barefoot all over, fastern a jack-rabbit thru sow thistle. Universalty stoogents was the first to do it, without no close on on the coldest day of the winter. No wonder they say them peeple is losing ther facultys. Wen pleece tried to arrest them on a charge of undeecent exposeyer they was unable to find on them any identifycation.

They even started doin these front-all assalts on yer TV. I mind seein' one runnin' behind Walter Crankhite wen he was intraviewing Mrs. Lady's Bird Johnson. He was sprised but she laffed to beet the band. I gess she has bin all over the world and seen many a forrin part. Sumbuddy even flash amung the Oscers at yer Cad-me Awards.

April Fool day was poplar with streekers. Durin yer Cheery Blossom Festeral sum dun it in fronta Warshing-ton's Monumental wile everybuddy sung "Yer Antsir Is Blowin' in the Wind". They was tryin to shame Precedent

Nixon into showing his private tape. I figgered he'd be smart to streek hisself across yer Whitehouse lawn to proove he wasn't all that crooked.

Canajuns wasn't too friggid to try it, and it wernt too long ago it happen in the middle of a pritty dull hocky game at yer MakeBeleeve Gardings. Our Leefs was losin' two aginst nuthin', and that's what this fella had on his plackerd wen he step out on the ice in his socks and that's all. I dunno wether his sine was bein' persnal or refurrin' to the score, but the cops chase after him. He run in and out of yer peanulty box, up passt yer golds, yer red, yer green and yer gray, but they finely corner him way up where they play with yer Nashnul Antrum and they grab him rite there by the organ.

Chapter 4.   1975

fer Yeer of Yer Wimmen's Rib

I dunno wen they started desecratin' differnt yeers for differnt reesons. Seemed to be 1975 wen alluva suddint wimmen wuz warin' buttons wich the guvmint started handin' out. I thot at first them Grits was havin' nuther leckshun becus the buttins sed "Why Not?" Valeda wore her whynot out to a soopymarkit that first week, and cum home so blame mad she slam it in the shiffrobe and never tuck it outa her drawers agin. Seems morn one smarty alec had cum up to her, seen the buttin and sed: "Why not, baby. Yer place or mine?" Now the wife, she's no Wimmen's Librium — if anything, she's Wimmen's Conserve and Preserve Maker — but she thinks this hole Wimmen's Yeer thing as run by the men in our guvmint was the biggest rip-off since the Eatin Cattlehog, and that wuz oney one page at a time.

This was the yeer sum entreprenhoor in Trontuh open up a topless shoeshine parlor, so's men cood look down on wimmen doin' ther meanyall tasks. At the same time, wimmen in yer thirdworld was bein' the prime minsters like Injura Gandy, Goldy My Ear, and Mrs. Bandersnatch of Seal-on.

Valeda sez they otta have had a buttin that sed "Why not knot?". She sez the way most yung peeples was tyin' the knot that yeer was not by gettin' into holy ackermony, but by the yung fella havin' a vastsextummy. Valeda even wanted me to have one. I tole her it wuz a case of lockin' the barn door after the stud has bin put to pastyer. But she aloud as she has allys wanted to give me sumthin' fer my berthday that she wooden have to dust off every weakend.

Mebby the best thing annybuddy dun for wimmen this yeer was erecktin' up yer CN Excommunication Tower, the world's tallest unsupported stricture. Them Roosians haz a hire one, but it has strings atttached. So ours is number one on yer hite parade. Valeda wood never go up on it cuz she gits a bit dizzy when she wares arch supports. But she still approves of this big put-up job durin' Intynashnul Wimmen's Yeer.

She thinks yer CN Tower was erected up fer to teech the simble-minded men of Canda humititty. So far it hasn't took. Valeda thinks all this talk about wimmin bein' equal with men is nonsents. She hopes it never happens in our famly becuz fer her it'll be a awful step downhill.

I guess the big-name Libber this year was MarGrit Terdo, altho she dint reely do the big brake-away till '77. But she sure come on strong at yer Come-in-yerwealth Confluence in yer West Undies. They was all over the place, Houndyerass, Guyanus, Jamoca and even among yer Cubists. One nite MarGrit got up and sung a little song wich she had decomposed all by herself, both yer words and yer leericks, and it was all about wat a reel Muther she had becum, and how Pee Air took his turn helpin' her with the kids, and even housework. Can't you jist see our Primer Minster hoovering around the livin' room at 24 SusSex Drive, and goin' thru the changes with them Pampers. My gol, if he dun all that he'd hardly have time fer to cleen out his cabnut.

Forners affares

We had a dustup with yer Yank that yeer over them Cubists. We dun sum bizness with Fiddle Casteroil, that beerdsmokin' seegar fella wears clothes like he's peeling pertaters at Camp Boredom. He wanted to give us the bizness of sellin' him sum injuns. I don't meen the Injuns what are our native peeples, I mean locomotions that pulls yer rolling stock. Seems that they is made in Canda but the cumpny has its pairnts in yer States and we is jist a branched plant. So the U.S. reprehensitivs of the cumpny sed we hadda git ther permission fer to sell them railcars, and they wuzn't gonna give it on accounta they suspected our locomotivations in doin' it.

Mind you, at the same time them Merkens was sellin' their stuff to them deepdide Reds in Roosia and China. Mind you, they wasn't gonna force us, them Yanks. Jist slap our wrists a bit and then take a hands off altitude. I herd that when a pairnt cumpny gits in trubble it's yer branched plant is the first to git the axe, but I think cutting ther hands off is jist a bit drastick.

Anuther thing happen across our inoffensive border this yeer was wen New York State tried to take over our nashnul embloom. All of a sudden they started sayin that their simble was yer beever. Now yer French word fer beever is Castor, and the reeson we have always took off our hat to it, is that Castor oil was wat got our country movin'. And fer them Yanks to give us heet fer tryna trade with Fiddle Casteroil, and then try and skin us out of our own homegroan beever!

Roylty

There was more flutterin about the visit of yer world's most illegible batcheler than anythin' else in this wimmin's yeer. Talk about Mickey Jaggy and his Running Stones, he didn't have no more groopiers than this royl lad. Wen he went to yer Reedo Halls Balls every yung debutramp in the country was tryna cut in. He seem to spend most of the evenin dancin' with Marg Terdo. I guess he figgered she was safe enuff to hang around, bein' a married woman with her feet parrlell to the ground, and sum munths gone to boot. He sed he hadda be careful hoo he rubs noses with. Mebby that's why he finely run away frum it all and got up to Ellsmear Island fer to fish thru the ice with sum Artick chars, insted of hanging around yer Shadow Lorryay and fishin' thru the ice fer the marciano cherries. He sure had a good time under yer Artick ice in his Scooberubber soot, proovin' I sposse that he was Prints of all the Whales.

A lotta peeple was disappoint wen he went back home single. The wife and former sweetheart, she is of Scotch distraction, and she was kinda hopin' that Bony Prince Charlie wood hook up with our own Florry Macdonald like his predatorsucksessor dun a coupla hundert yeers ago. We cooda maid him Guverning Genral, and I've always felt Florry would make a ringtail snorter of a prime minstress. We coulda had Charlie in the Hall and Flora on the floor.

One of the reesons he mebby hadda hurry home was that the Queen was runnin outa Royaltys. Bleeve it er not she was findin' it hard fer to keep up with the Joneses over there with her Buckinghams Palace, Sandwidgeham and that hole shootin match up in Scotland fer to grouse about, yer BallMorals. And you'd be sprised at the things she has to pay out. Yer Household Calvary and yer Coldcream Guards and the rest of them Palissaids, her rod and her staff fer to comfort her.

She don't have wat you'd call a workin' famly neether, sept fer that bruther-in-law that flashes his Brownie. And with little Princess Annie married to whatsizname won't be long before they'll be heerin' around the place the pattern of tiny hooves. Her Majestic has got more declared dependence than Richer Nixon ever dreemt up.

Hocky

I mind the time wen fer to be good in hocky you hadda skate good and score goals. I was brot up on yer Kidline of Primo, Joe Bushy Jackson and Charlee Connacker, back in yer dirty thirties, wich wern't so dirty in hocky as nowadaze. Nobuddy wuz out there fer to haffassissinate the uther, sept mebby wen Eddie Shore aced Bailey the oncet, and they never let him fergit it. Nowadaze they start swingin ther sticks high in grade fore. And no wonder! How would you feel if sumbuddy woke you up to practiss hocky at three oclock in the mornin', wich is the oney time them little midges kin git on the ice. If anybuddy ast me to git up in the middla the nite and start the chores, I mite cremate sum mayhemp too. And sum of them kids aint playin' fer almamatter anymore; they're playin' fer allamony. They wanna git pade off fer ther goals with ten speed CCF bikes and potable TVs.

38

I hate to say this, but I think that all this trubble start when yer NHL was considered expandable and dubbled ther size, and hadda compeet with yer copshows on U.S. teevee. Mebby this is why Premeer Billy Davis of Ontario got Judo LaMarsh, our Stately Seckertairy that was, hired fer to keep the violins offa TV. The wife she got upset wen she heered this, on accounta she jist loves that Al Churnme whanging his bow over his fiddle on that Tommy Humper show. But that wernt the kinda violins they was talkin' bout. They meen the Mafiascos of yer Cosy Nostril with ther snub masheen gums. It seems the guvmint wants to take violents offa the TV and the hockyrink and put it back where it belongs — in the home. And they dun it too. Fer this was the yeer that ther was a new quiz show brung to TV, "Questing Peeriod", wich brung a rashin of parlymentry bludshed into yer livinroom fer one hour a day.

Penulty Box: Rooskies 2 — Canajuns 5

Kulcher

Yer *Deepthrote* was the pitcher that maid the most munny this yeer. Our boy Orville tried to git to see it. He thot it wuz one of those Walt Dizzly pictures about a jeraff with larryinjiteass. We luv all them Dizzly pitchers, like *Mary Pop-in* and *Titty Titty Gangbang*. But *Deepthrote* terned out to be what they call fornography, feecherin' lotsa oriole sex. I don't even know wat that is, but Valeda sez it's all them birds gettin' together and talkin' about it after.

I once seen one of them babybloo moovies on the laidlaid show in Trontuh. When the villin come at the girl with a pilluh, I thot sure he wuz gonna assfixyate her, but it tern out he jist put it under her bullocks. I gess she had trubble in her lumber reegions. Valeda tern it off afore I cood see what happen nex — probly sum kinda fizzlyo-therappy — but it sure look like more fun than beatin' sombuddy up like on them copshows.

Morls

Pre-martial sex wuz giv the go ahed this yeer by the First Laidy of yer Benightied States, Beddy Ford. The wife pert neer choke on her puff weet wen she reed about Beddy allowin' as how her dotter wuz havin' a candlestine affair with some yung dood, and she wern't goin' to intyfeer. You gotta give her credit fer makin' out that honesty is the best pollyticks.

I dunno if her husband, Geritol, was so happy about all this book of revelation she was openin' up. I think his dotter's virginity was too much to lose after Veet Napam. Seemed like from then on Resident Ford kep falling all over hisself. He went over to Spain after the devalidation of yer Franco to take the Spanish fly past. On his way home he got offa plane which flew down among yer Canarys, then he got out fer a pee-stop and fell flat on his A-sores. But he'd jist pick hisself up and start all over agin, sayin' that our trubbles was over and we was outa the woods at last. Sounds more to me like we was up the crick. There was all kinds of roomers down to Warshinton and more plots than a semitairy. First the C.I. of A. was sposed to be after Jack Anderson, a weakly communist frum yer *Warshinton Post*, and then there was Squeaky Frump, one of Charlie Manson's Angels, who tried to put violents back on the TV by takin' a potluck shot at Ford. I sumtimes think all of these half-assassinators wooden a dun it if they cooda bin on camera therselves as a contesterunt on "Let's Make a Deal". Up here in Canda, we can't go off half-cock all that easy becuz we got no garntee to bare arms in our billy rites, and a good thing too. Down there they got a foul piece for every two and half peeple, and owin' to that fack, there gits to be morn more half peeple every yeer.

Uppin the air

This was the premeer yeer of Mirrorbell, Muntryall's second airport that was sposed to take it out of the pas-tyeer and into the fewcher. Seems to me they'd bin better off leevin' it a pastyer. They tride to do the same thing to us over to Pickaring, Ontaryo. They took a queezibility studdy that found out they didden need a secund airport after they had got up yer Interminable Number Two at Malton. But that didn't stop yer federasts up to Ottawa. They seem determine to have anuther freeasco to go with the one in Cuebeck.

So they bot up thousandsa acres of prime farmland which wood be assfaulted. Well sir, the lokels got up in ther arms about this, and everybuddy sined a partition agin it. And the vox of yer peeples won over the bull frum yer Common House. Seems the pervincials under Billy Davis wooden go infra structures like soors and skeptical tanks and roads that they needed fer to git the airport under its own steam.

So the good lokel ladies have stopped lyin' down in front of them bulldosers fer to save ther homes, becuz them big jets won't be comin' over ther feekels and scarin' ther cows by breakin' thru the wind barrier. But as sumbuddy once sed, the price of peece is eternal vigilantys, and I wooden be sprised if them burrocraps tride this hole nit-pickering idee agin.

Other things was up in the air this yeer. In 1967 Nash-nully Offensive Minster Pall Hellyer had eunuchficated the Armed Servicers by makin' them all ware the one uniform, wich made them all look like they was clectin' parkin' tick-ets. Sum of them Admirables was so upset they went down with ther penshuns. But they got the Hellyer outa there, and in '75 they had a new Offensive fella, Jim Richardson, and he tride to rettero-act them stand-in orders and bring back seppertism in yer farces. I dunno what happend to all this turnin' back yer crock, there's still rumblins amung yer Three-Armed Farces.

UFO's was still up in the air this yeer and I don't meen yer United Farmers of Ontario. Sum scoller out in Elberta got hisself a fat LIP grant fer to rite a book about them Unindemnifiable Flyin' Objecks, all the sites that evrybuddy has bin seein' amung yer constipations of yer Milkyway. More peeple had bin catchin site of extra testial frisbees and this yeer come out a explication fer sum of them. They showed on TV a flyin sasser what had bin bilt by sum desinin' peeple up to yer Olivier de Havilland works. She had a diafram morn twenty feet across with two fellas sittin in it doin' ther jet repulsions. And that's what them utter spaced out beleevers had bin seein' — a Hoovercraft shape like a cowflap.

This yeer's big no-show wern't no comet but the Mr. Nood Tronto contest. Mebby it was a way of celibating Wimmen's Year but nothin' come off. Cross my hart and hope to spit, they planned to prade these fellas in ther bareskins down to yer Pally Royale wher Bert Noisey's band used to swing. They called Bert Canda's King of Swing, and I sposed they were using his old hang-out ter to try to find a new one. Now I've had a bareskin pitcher took of me, but I was lying' on it, and I was oney three munths old. I think a nood weddin' mite come off, tho'. It'd sure be easy to see who was yer best man.

Missyun Unpossible happen this yeer in utter space when yer Yank asternuts and yer Serviet comicsnuts teemed up in yer statusfear. They was both blown up frum ther respectibble bases but they met together above every- thing and shook hands and visited eech other's crapsules. It did seem a shame that the big Two hadda git that high before they cood start to co-opulate with eech other.

Scandles

Premeer Terdo was give a 100 proof car cost 83 thousand dollar fer to keep out yer bullets, but the thing that maid the big splash was his swimming pool. (Not in the car, altho' it sure look big enuff.) Terdo din't pay fer the car nor the pool, but nobuddy begrudge him the car. A lotta peeple wunderd if the biznessmen hoo give Pee Air this expansive seepage in his basement cood be accuse of influence piddling. Mebby they figgered it wooden be noticed in a swimming pool. His wife Marg was give a two-thousand-dollar camera by King Insane of Jordan so she cood studdy fornography.

Sum peeple thot it was a scandle this yeer wen they got upped more fer ther milk. Me bein' a primary perjuicer mite sound like speshul bleeding on my part, but I kin tell ya rite now it's the muddleman gits mosta that increase that you hadda pay fer yer children's milk. Bleeve me, there's a lotta muddlin' men between your tots and our teets. I think a bigger scandle was them Common House MPs votin' therselves a 50 percent raze radio-active to last July. But that's becum a anal festeral by now. Yanks thot that Premeer Blakeninny was a bit of a Sassakatchewan Ruf- frider wen he tuck over ther potash stash and sed "Wat's mines is ours." He cot them with our plants down and they bin that way ever sints.

Yer Injun brotherhood thot it was a scandle that them oily cumpnees never settled ther abridge-in-all rites wen they stake out a gas pipeline up in yer friggid waste. So the Nashnul Elegy Bored started up a freezability studdy.

The wife thot it was a scandle wen she herd the

Geritol Ford keepin' his hed above Watergate

Guvmint put money into Sin Crude. She thot it was anuther moovy like yer *Deepthrote*. But it was us loanin' a buncha oil tyfoons a haffa billyun dollar fer to lick the tar sands.

Others thot the biggest scandle of 1975 was the lettin' off of Henry Morgan's Tailer, who wasn't in coats and pants like he sounds, but was a mediccle man practicin' mostly on kitchen tables. The guvmint let him off scotch free becuz he'd bin doin what they do all the time — avoidin' the issue. But Terdo had alreddy passed his movemint on the floor of yer Common House in '68 sayin' the guvmint cood not do its bizness in yer bedroom, and that even homeosectionals cood have abortions.

44

Egonomicks

Fer yer John Q. Rapepayer 1975 was sure a funny yeer. Not funny ha-ha, funny finger down yer throat. John Turner was in charge of all our fisical affairs that yeer and in Joon he finely give a publick accounting of hisself. He seemd a mite nerviss at wat he was presentin us with. His upper lips kep puffing in and out like he was blowin' on a trumpet that wern't there. And there sure wern't much to blow about wen he got thru. He upped us fer the gas agin, and he made it harder fer youngfoke fer to git a low-crossed house. Turner felt we was luckier'n yer Yank, who had bin recessed and depressed fer the last six munths. If we was doin' so good then why did he resine hisself a cup-pla munths later if we was in such mint condishun? Sum peeple thot he mite even cross the floor and becum the gratest Tory ever sold. But he went and sat on his little back bench till he cood git hisself a Bay window office fer to practice with his privates sextors. Mind you, I don't think Turner ever wanted to be in Infernal Revenue in the first place. He'd a bin happier with yer Externals' Affairs. But the main disagreemint tween Turner and Terdo was over wether they shood control therselves. You mind that was the big issyuh tween Stanfeeled and Terdo in last yeer's lection. Well sir, a weak later, Banana Bob up and quit. A lotta peeple has since sed he wernt good enuff fer federast pollticks but a lot of uthers has kep wunderin' if all that "Merry Charisma" nonsense was good enuff fer him. Uth-ers held his famly's undyware aginst him, thinkin' he never made if frum yer bottoms up. Mebby that was his trap-door. But Stansfeeled was a first rate menstrator wen he ran things in Nose Kosher, but he never got the chants to show his stuff up yer Reed-O. Still, his integrititty stuck out like sore thums.

But the funny thing was as soon as Banana Bob had slipped out, Premeer Terdo dun a switchy-about and brung in Stansfeeled pricey wage controls. I bleeve it was Thanksgivering weak-end wen Terdo all of a sudden come on the TV. You cooden watch nothing else, he had our tubes tied up fer the nite. I was jist havin' a bite of my secund peece of punkin pie wen alluva sudden he shout "Tite-in yer Belt!" I pert neer threw up. Then he told us that he was anointin' this lady Perl Bumtree fer to be the Fud Prices Revue Broad. Him and her was gonna rassle inflammation to the ground. Terned out he cooden even rassle Perl Bumtree to the ground.

'Bout this time the Terdos had ther therd Blessid Event, to go along with little Sashay and Justin Time. Wood have bin nice to pull off the hat trick agin but she shelled out before HelloWean. Everybuddy hoped he wood give the country the same kinda plannin' he give his famly, but uthers still bleeved in a mirrorcull.

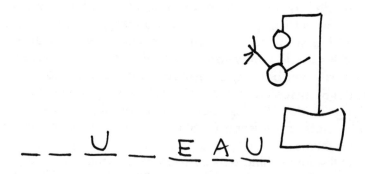

_ _ <u>U</u> _ _ <u>E</u> <u>A</u> <u>U</u>

Chapter 5.　　　　　1976

Yer Yeer of Yer Limpricks Games

1976 was to be Canda's yeer "in the Eyes and Eers of
yer Wirld". Never mind that yer Yank was havin' off his
Bisextennial, that little Mare frum Muntryall Jeans Dropout
was deetermin to put his town on the map fer all posteerier
ages. Wen he was ast where all the munny was comin
frum, little Jeans jist smile enematickly and sed: "Yer
Limpricks kin no more loose munny than a fella kin git
preggerunt." Well sir, in wreckrowspeck it looks to me like
our little Mare faled the rabbids test, fer yer Limpricks
wound up a billion-dollar baby with a 600 millyun doller
defickate.

That big Irish Pier, Lord Killanolin, wat was in charge
of yer Limprick end, he kep comin' over here and smilin'
and sayin' everything was as hunky as a dory. But fer a
time there, yer Big-Domed Stayjum wern't gonna be
availabull fer the opening torching, and they was gonna
have to use the Bellydrome, wat was bilt fer yer sex-day
bike races.

Carryin' the torch itself end up costin' half a millyun
dollars. Why din't they fone up the Consoomer's Gas and
have em do it fer free? Even yer CBC wooden dare put out
a pilot that cost that much. But yer Limprick Cumitty, they
cooden be satisfy with a lowcal lite fer to start things off
with a bang. Oh no, they hadda go all the way over to yer
Grease fer to git ther old flame.

They started off over there on Mount O'Limp hard by
yer Tempels of Hernia. I dunno how you start a fire up top
of a mounting. I spose they dun it by rubbing two Geek Boy
Scouts together. Then she was relaid down yer mounting
by 520 Geeks relaying eech other 520 times till they
reeched yer Crappolis, an old bank bildin in the rundown
part of Athins. I thot, my gol, if ther gonna run this thing by

hand frum Grease to Muntry-all she won't be there till we're in our Gay Cups.

But now cum yer trikky parts. Insted of sendin' off that flame by ornery male (wich wood have bin even longer than gittin' it off by hand), they got one of them Geek Sensers. I don't meen the kind wat reeds everybuddy's male, or counts heds fer the federasts. This senser is sumthing that takes that flame and puts it into elocution in frunt of a speshul pairabollocks mirror, and lionizes yer partickles so's that it casts a reflection on a raddio siggunal whenver it gits the impulse, and beems itself up to one of them satellyites that are furever circumsizing the erth.

So this thing is travlin' up there in yer permamint fermamint, till it's brung down to erth by the same kinda touch tellyfone you has if yer a prinsess. But do she cum down hard by yer Limprick Stayjum? Oh no. I gess mebby yer Geek cooden throw her that far, fer she was transmut to a big wide reseever antenema in Millvilledge, Nova's Kosher. Now she is relaid by landline tellyfone to yer Parlymint Hill missin' Muntryall by a cuppla hundert mile! No wunder it cost a haffa millyun once them federasts got into the act. And they got a flame of ther own goin' all the time rite in front of ther Common House, neer yer Toom of yer Unnoan Lobbyist. I dunno wat kind of flame it is. Mebby the reeson they din't use it is becuz it wuz not sakered but propain.

Lazer Flashers

But first the flame has to git decode and cleered by yer Securatitty peeple at yer Nova Kosher end. After yer Moonick freeasco they was strong on the lookout fer terrierasts and sabbathoors. Then it gits sent up to Ottawa by a lazy beem — that's sorta a flashlite in heet — and this starts a fire in yer Ottawa uren. That's what rich peeple calls a voz, a uren. Then Premiere Terdo was call upon to dip the wick of his torch at 3 o'clock July 15, and *pouf* the whole rangdangdoo wood start off with a bang. D'ye see why she cost haff a millyun dollar? Don't you think Pee-Air cooda dun jist as well with a flick of his Bick?

48

And that ain't all. We still hadda git that flame to yer Doomed Stayjum in Muntryall. They needed about 230 splinters fer to carry the torch all that way. Yer splinter is a fella kin run fast fer sum time. Nowadaze they call them jogglers. And this is where Canajuns tuck up ther parts. Premeer Terdo was to hand that flamin' torch—the wife was worried he wooden known wich end was up—to the first of 230 voluntairyairy runners who was eech to run a killyermeter (wich is a mile after inflayshun).

To git on this relayerself teem you hadda be able to run yer killyermeter in lessen five minit. Not oney that, but you hadda have five fiscally fit frends fer to take yer place in case you dropout by the wheyside. Valeda wanted me fer to have the honner of doin' that, but I tole her I oney had four fit frends and I was savin' them fer to be my paul-barers. I spose it helps if you blongs to a sports club like yer Vic Tansy, but the oney sport club I ever blonged to was yer Crownbrand Siruppy bunch run by West McNite over the raddio. And you didden git nuthin' fer it, you know. Wen the guvmint says volumetairy they meen it. You pays fer yer own beddenbored. All you got fer showin yer huffinpuffinstuff was a paira sneekers, a tee shirt and a sweatband. I thot that was an orkestry that plays wile you perspire, but it's sumthin you wares over yer hed fer to keep yer pores close. The tea shirt had COJO writ all over it. You mind him, he was the baldhedded poleese fella used to suck his lollyspop on the TV. I dunno wat he hadda do with our Limpricks eggsept that he's a Geek too.

Flag De-Bait

Now you think after all that ruckus it wood be simple jist to lite up and tie one on. But "Taiwan Off" was more like it, fer even before any athaletes feats started there was a big catterwall about hoos flag was up and hoos flag is down. There hadden bin sich a flag to-do since Lesley Piercin let the Union jack off our pole. You mind wen everybuddy ignored yer Red Chinamen with ther undivide attenshun? Well, this time they was doin' it to yer uther Chinee, hoo wanted to be called yer Republicans of China,

His or hernya?

50

but them Commonests on yer Maneland I spose hated the idee of bein' libelled as Demmycraps.

I'll betcha there wern't no such tenpest in a peepot wen they held yer first Limprick games back in 400 B.B.C. First of all there was no place to stick a flagpole in the big prade on accounta every one of them Geek athaleets was bare as bird. Not even so much as a jocular strap. In them days them Geeks wood drop everything every four yeers and hed fer the games. And wen they was tired frum bein' in ther heets, they'd jist reetire to an Olive's grove and rest on ther lorrels. And they din't have to wait till after to know wether they'd scored, fer they cood go up to the Temple of Essoffaguss, where they had yer Delsick Orifice. This was a tempelwoman hoo sat on a hole of hot air, and went into a transom wen peeple ast her wat the odds was. I wisht Jeans Dropout wooda had sumone like her wen he was figgerin' out his esttimits.

It was yer Roamin dressed up yer Limpricks a bit by makin' them all ware yer tokeus. Mind you, them Roamin turn it into a regler sircuss by havin' yer Christian play the Lions Club wile Impurer Neero made a fool of hisself by Fiddlin' on the Roof. After them Roamins got thru there wern't no more games fer 1600 yeer. It jist seems that everytime that Games git over-orgynized they ends up red-taped and tied up in knots.

The first Geek games was start up fer to stop a war. Fer a minit it look like yer '76 Limpricks in Muntryall was gonna end up by startin' one. New Zeeland sorta ruggered the hole thing up by playing with yer Apart Heds frum Souse Affricker. That cut out the big race everybuddy wanted to see, a 1500-heetmeeter tween a fella frum Tanzinsania and one down under in Ostertailyuh.

But the games *did* git started, and the wife and I was tied to our toobs the hole two weeks insted of gittin' in the hay. I thot I wood git sick to deth of twelve, mebby furteen, hour a day of runnin', jumpin' and divin', but Valeda and Orville and I becum a buncha vidiotic nuts watchin' them brake the records they bin sittin' on fer four yeers.

And it sure change my idee of wat a athaleet wuz. I thot it was sum big fella bilt like a blacksmith hoo wood give yez a hermia jist to look at him. But after yer '76 games I cum to the concussion that yer Wirled of Sport is under the thum of sum fourteen-yeerold girls. And I don't meen jist that Roomanyun teenyflopper, Naggyuh Cummineat, hoo flipped everybuddy by hangin' around the uneven bars in Muntryall. We had sum teenyagers of our own, up ther with the best of them. You take that Nantsy Waterpick, the little Helluvagoanian, I pert neer had a backstroke watchin' her, but it sure was a nice change frum all them pollytishuns backstrokin' eech other. Then there was sum boat racey girls, I don't even mind ther names, slappin' ther skulls in the water. They was called the pair without cox, but they don't have to explane the facks of life to me.

We gotta cuppla Sliver medals and mebby enuff bronz fer to do a paira baby shoes, but we never hit the golds the way them East Germs did. A lotta newspaperporters wuz askin why we wernt more meddled, but my gol if you live in a socialite country yuh git sudsiddy-ized like yew was a national reeshorse. Them Commonists, they don't bleeve in God, so they hasta bleeve in sumthin, so they bleeve in havin' a fizzicle fit. But they'll go so far as to give ther peeples horemones that'll sumtimes make ther sex life go thru the changes. Sumtimes you'd need a vet fer to tell the boys frum the girls. I seen one big Serviette watelifter feller cooda dun with one of yer 18-hour braws. He probly went home with his gold meddle, and sat around in fronta the stove, wooden even go to the store fer his muther. Them Athaletes over to yer Serviet Onion is treeted like moovy stars. I'd sooner have a nice modess young feller wood hang around the barn and help his muther with the milkin when she needs to lift her big cans.

Uther Pollyticks

Premeer Terdo starts off every yeer by dropping a brick with his Yeerend messyedge. This yeer he musta had a vote of overconfidents frum the confidents men in his

52

party, becuz he cum out agin yer free enterprize and was thinkin' of goin' out in a big way with yer capitalist's punishment. He seem to feel that the corpulent way of runnin' things was better. And he thru a big party fer the openin' of that new airport, yer Mirrorbell, where they pored shampane the way the contracters musta pored concreet fer to bild the place. And this was the yeer the guvmint spent two hunnert thousand doller watching poltroons at yer Nashnul Artysenter in Ottawa goin' to the bathroom. They timed how long it took peeple fer to take ther pee brakes during ther nocturnal intermishuns. Don't ast me why them timestuds stop-watched all this. Nobuddy's ever found out yit, but this was order by experks hoo are sposed to be outstanding in ther feeled. I'm outstanding in my feeled too, but that's becuz it's too far to go back to the house.

The Retrogressive Preservatives had ther Anal Convenshun in Febyouairy. Bob Stansfeeled din't have no Dalton Cramp at his side like wen they dun in John Doofenbeeker. He went P.C.fully like the gennelman he allus was. Meself, I was parshul to that Florry Macdonald. I figgered everybuddy in this country was reddy fer a Prime Mistress, but the upshat of it all was a unnoan by name of Joke Lark

This was the yeer that Cabnut Minster Andy Outlet got let out. He was in charge of yer Consooming Affairs and he wanted to refine down the price of shuggar, so he had Budge Dreary, yer Minster of Pubic Works, fone up the judge fer to make shure them shuggar barns dint git offa the hook fer playin Monopply. Tern out Outlet was give the hook insted fer intyfeerin with the cause of justice gittin' its own desserts.

Keeth Spicy hoo was in charge of yer buylingamalism amung yer sibilant serpents fessed up that them perversion corses they was puttin them thru wasn't worth a pinch of kooflap. He thinks it'd be better to do it amung yer yung. Meself, I think they shood start with the teenyagers fer the one sure way fer to lern a langridge is to fall in luv with a Garlic person. And if you wanna make time in Cuebec, you have to be abel to say "Quel hoor Estelle?"

That lection they had in Cuebeck cum November tern out to be the upsat of yer yeer. Roebear Bouracic he figgered he'd git a shoe in over that little Reamy Leveckyou, who last time cooden even hold onto his seet. But wen everybuddy axercise ther frenchfries it was them Separators wat got in. They called therselves yer Partly Cuebecwuzzes, but by hinkus they was now yer hole thing, and it was yer Libreeal Bourassic was the wuz-been. And it wern't yer langridge bizness, that Bill 222 of Boorassic's that was the hedake this time. Bourassic's slowgun was "three hundirt thousand new posishuns!" He was hopin' to git in by offrin' everybuddy a job up to yer Shames Bay Hydra. But peeple thot he was puttin out a sax manual, and they din't bleeve him fer one little bit. From now on them federasts will be havin' to mined ther PQs.

Yer Gondeleers of the Air struck hard this yeer fer to preserve the Garlic langridge in their cock pits. Most comtrollers told them to "Take off, ay!" and the Minister in Transports OttoPack Lang he tole them to keep flying in Limbo till the guvmint got off a report. He sed he was mostly worried about the safety asspex. Passengers dint know witch langridge to yell in: jist plane "Help!" or "Oh Sick Hoors!"

Merken affairs

The Ewe Ass had a dubble feecher this year, a 200-year analversry and a lection fer Precedent. The primer marys give the nod to ther present encumbrance Geritol Ford, but he had became this by being anointed by the old Trickydick, so he was puttin' hisself on the line fer to be counted. His oppsit nummer was a new fella to me, Carter. The only Carter I had heerd of down there was the inventer of yer Carter's little lover pills. But this 'un look like he never needed no pills. He had a smile I haven't seen since they tuck the stains offen our pianna. You'd swear he had morn 32 teeth; I wooden be sprize if sum of them wasn't Chicklets. Oney trubble he got into was wen he got intravude in Huge Heffer's maggyzeen, *Plowboy*, and admit that he had lust in his heart fer uther wimmen. He's lucky to

Leveck greets Terdo

keep it up there in the one place. Most uthers' lust kinda moves around.

The fella that had the most trubbles in yer Ewe Ass guvmint, Wane Haze, hoo was found in Congers with his sexretarry, who was a good tipe even tho she coodent. He clames he kep her around in a pivotall posishun whenever he got shorthanded. This is not to be confuse with Wilbermills, who kep chasin' after Foxy's Fanny, feedin' her guvmint shampane and hopin' to get her to vote on Proposishun One. He hopes to do to her what he be doin' to the taxpayers. Haze wuz in charge of yer Hazy Means Cummittee — name after him, no dout — and the thing thretten to tern into a kinda Waterbed Gate. Not that we haven't had this kinda hanky stanky up to Ottawa oursels. You mind, we had Gertie Mudslinger presentin' her breefs to Cabnut.

55

Over in Angland, they had some peckadildoes too with Christine Keelover and Mandy Rice-Krispees. But we all know that them pollytishuns make strange fellows in bed!

But the thing wat went on the hole of yer 76 was yer Ewe Ass celibation of ther Bisextenniel. Mind you they started blowin' out their candles haffway thru '75, before they was two hunnert yeerolds. Once they was with us as one of the further out parts of yer Berdish Rumpire, witch was persided over at the time by George yer Tird. But it was him put the kybo on them Colonials, by puttin' tacks in ther tees and ternin them all into Republickans. They sed "Up Yer Union, Jack!" and went into Congers with eech other and cum out with ther own Billy Rites, called yer Declaration fer yer Dependents. Mind you, them Berdish din't give up without a fite. It started up at Archie Bunker's Hill and went as fur as Lexington and Concurd, where a lotta peeple got hurt. Musta bin one bizzy intersexion. One of the early paterotics got cot in this jam was Nate Inhale, who becum dead and famous at the same time fer sayin' the famous quote: "I'm jist as glad I have oney one life fer to give to the country." George Warshinton staid alive by forgin' fer hisself in the Valleys, and sleeping around the hole country till he becum the father of it. And wen he thru a silver doller across yer river, the Berdish lost the toss. Mind you, a doller went a lot further in them days. But wen the Berdish squares formed up under Lord Cornhole-Us, the Yanks jist laffed at them. Them Yankys din't have no unyforms, jist Lindsay Woolen frum yer Goodwill, wile them Berdish was dress up fit to kill: tite white briches, silk stockins,ruffied shirts and fancy white Dynel whigs. The Yanks dint know whether to fite them or take them to a dinner-dance. The Berdish was so well tricked out, they figgered they wood extinguish therselves in battel, but when they formed up in ther pantaloons, they fell never to rize agin.

Them Yanks as wuz pro-Berdish was called Torys and cum across to our side, our first batcha draft dodgers. We mite a bin celibatin' this hollyday along with yer Yank, becuz durin yer War that we won 18-12, most Canajuns din't care much witch country they blonged to. It was a case a haff a dozen a one and a six pack of the tother. But do you know who riz the biggest stink about the Yank comin' up and evading them? It was yer Cuebec-wuzzes that dun the most to fite off yer StarStripers and staid loyl to ther Berdish King. Sure makes you think, don't it, fer to reelize that the oney thing wat held our country together in them daze was our French conneckshun!

Chapter 6.   1977

Yer Yeer of Yer Sepperato

Yer seprater of yer yeer fer 1977 was not Reamy LeVeckYou but Mar Grit Trousseau. Funny thing was the hole thing happen on her weddin' analversery. Up til that time nobody had a ninklin of trubble up yer SusSex Drive. Hadden she bin on the shampain trail with Pee Air and sayin' how much she luvved the guy?

All of a suddint ther she was in Trawntuh a woopin' it up in an all-nite club with Micky Jaggy and his Galling Stones. I don't mind them partickler rotten rollers but my boy Orville sez that ther kind of a wild beetle hoo cant git no status fractions. I noe yer Premiere Pee Air takes to that kinda stuff fer I seen him on the TV shakin' hisself out and about in one of them trade schools, wat they call yer Disco Tech.

There was Mar Grit in the middle of this diskyteck snappin' her Brownie with a hot flash and leavin' no Stone unterned. The day that cum out in the papers it was pert neer impassible fer to git a fonecall in Metropoppolitan Parry Sound, fer all the wimmen in the districk was leavin' ther cold frames and sittin' on ther hot seats by the party line fer to find out wat was goin' on. The wife and former sweethart, Valeda, she even plaid one of our boy Orville's Galling Stones reckerds fer to find out wat kinda musick dun this to yer Premeer's wife. She cooden git no stratus-faction frum it neether. Sed it sound like a coupla skeltons makin' out on a tin roof in a hale storm. And Micky Jaggy's singin' sound to her like wat our coalie does outside wen he wants to git in on yer nite of a full moon.

Well, the Shakespeer sez musick has charms fer to smooth yer savidge brests, but Marg Trousseau's bayin' at the moon sure ster up a tempissed. Her husbin, he never sed a thing, give er take a black eye, when his flower child

58

went all to seed.

Marg and Pee Air becum our leading seppartists cum Joon. Marg started up a hole new buncha careers. First there was fornograffy, wich she studded at Stewdeeyo 54 in New York. Nuthin' much develop outa that. Then she becum a nactress in fillums. She dun this the twice, but I think the perjuicers kep the films and releesed her. It was Boney Prince Charlie first tole her to fritter her glitter on yer sliverscrean. The wife thinks she otta have bin at Strattferd insted, playin' yer titel roll in *Much Todo About Nuthin*.

Housewife of yer Yeer

The wimmen round my parts all seem to blaim Marg fer all these martial trubbles over yer SusSex Drive. They felt she had went from bein a rose in his lapell and worked her way down to be a thorn in his side. But I see it all start

59

up by the huzbin, fer I mind the time this yeer when Terdo cum down to yer Universally of Trawntuh, wich was goin' thru tuff times. Like me, they was not in possessun of all of ther facultys and was findin' it tuff fer to place ther stoogents in jobs after they was granulated. Pee Air was give sum kinda honorarium decree that day — I think he's up fer yer third degree — and he tole yer stewdint bodies that if they coodn't git a job in Canda they shood hit out fer the States. Oney person took his advice was his own wife.

Udder Sepperators

Anuther new kinda Sepperator, cum up this yeer was yer Westerner. I bin around Sepperators fer morn thirty five yeer, man and beest, and never had any trubble with them, but wen they starts to go, all that centralfrugal action kin make you dizzy jist watchin' it.

But my gol there's bin Seppraters out West ever since they got frate-raped by yer CPR. Wat seems to bother a lotta Westers nowadaze is yer French conneckshun, and I don't mean them dopey pushers in the moovys, but all them Franklyfoned Cabnut Minsters hoo seem to be a power-house in yer Commonhouse. Us here in Uppity Canda kinda feels baffled in the middle between them Steeryo Sepperates. If yer Western stile Sepperators ever gits fully slated, summers between yer Retrogressive Preservative and yer Sociable Credit Cards, this country of ours mite git ruptured three ways. This is wat they call gittin' BallCan-ized, and if that ever happens we'll jist fall one by one into the waitin' arms of — no, not yer Benighted States, they got enuff trubbles with ther own Sepperator down to PoorToe Reekio and up yer Pannamaniacs Canal. Nossir, we'll git picked off by them Malted Nashnul Corpulations like yer Ixxon, Texassco yer IBUM and yer Inty Nashnul Tell-a-Tell. Watever the Seprators try to reeson with me, all I kin think of is the "Divide Up and Conk You" bizness thunk up by that Mongoloid fella Ganges Can when he led his tarty hords all the way frum yer Gobye dessert rite up yer Tur-key to the gaits of Standbull.

Thing that bothers me is yer French conneckshun tween Terdo and Leveckyou. Seems to me they is link up with eech other in a kind of parry-mewchull survival kit. The one of them both needs the tother fer to keep the pubelick's minds offa unemploymint and the cost of keepin' up livin', jist likes them Arbs needs Izzreel fer to have sumthin' in common fer to keep them togither aginst. Canajuns was startin' to think that the oney way they cood unite ther country, was to have all the provinshuls gang up agin yer federasts in Ottawar.

One Western sepperator hoo stood out frum the resta his party was that not so little Jack Horner, hoo cum out of his corner, turned his coat, and sed, "Wat a good buy am I." Terdo put him on display in yer Cabnut as a Minster without no PoorFoolyo. Ther was loud screems frum yer Tory wen he defecated over tother side, and becum a True Grit. I think Big Jack was jist gruntled after he lost that "Take Me to yer Leedership" Race at yer Tory prevention that yeer, to young Joe Cluck, hoo sideswiped everybuddy incloodin' Flory yer Red Mennis Macdonald, Big Clod Fognair, and Pall Hellion, hoo was anuther disgrunt Grit. Not to menshun yer hotshot out-front favrit, bilingamal Briney Bullroney.

Jack was took into yer Shadder Cabinet, wich is the top members of yer Opposit Position in the jobs they hopes to git fer reel, but I gess he jist got tired of livin' in the shadders with young Joe. Mebby it was becuz Joe married that young Mactier girl and she refuse to tag on his slurname. That sorta Wimmen's Librium wood rankle yer ankles of our Jack, Canda's John Wane.

Joe hisself was bizzy gittin' his party defeet in five out of six byelerections. Them Tories is always cuttin' off ther nose to spike ther drink. Even Mizz MoeReen Macteer admit they is give to crappin' all over therselfs and in 1977 they was slidin' so fast down yer Gallup Pole they musta got callussed tween the laigs. Yer young leeder of yer Opposit posishun was gittin' lots of it frum inside his own party. It must be gory to be a Tory fer they don't seem to

61

bleeve in Follow the Leeder.

But I spose the creem of yer Sepperators is still yer Cuebeck moddle, Leveck. Nowadaze candied-dates don't git voted in so much as ther preevious encumbrances git voted out. But Reamy got in trubble pritty soon after he got in the driver's seat. It happen on a cold snowy nite in Muntryall when he was goin' downhill and got axadentally involve with a pedderastrian, who end up riggered with mortis. It all come to cort, and the witnesses fer the persecution sed that Reamy was drivin' down hill too fast, mebby forty mile a hour, wooda tuck him two hundert feet fer to stop propper. Yer defensive ones sed he wernt goin' haff that fast, and he stop within fifty feet. By the time yer trile got thru the jedge seem to feel that Reamy was park at the curb and this ded man thru hissel under the weels of his car. He got fine tho' — fifty doller fer not waring glasses. My gol, who needs glasses wen you got contacks like that?

Noobroom in Witehouse

There was a new precedent set down in Warshinton this yeer, a peenut farmer becum yer White Houser. He sprized everybuddy at his InHogRation by gittin' up offa his bubbledome lemonzeen and him and the wife hoofin' it all the way up the street fer to take his Oaf of Offus. And he kepp up yer common touch wen he made his first fireside chat jist like R.F.D. used to do back in his Depression. But Jimmy he dint have no frocked up coat and cutaway pants. He jist sat there in his old Carteriggan swetter and tole us his thermalstat was down blow yer '69. And he had calssified music playing on his background — Joehan Sebastian Backerack the wife sez — probly to drown out the sounds of his bruther Billy burpin' on beer.

Bout the only failyer he had that first munth in his Ovary Offus was rite back home in Plains, Gorgeous, his home town. Seems that they disintegrated the minister who tride to be a Christyun and let a black feller into one of the back seets. Jimmy went down there to cleer up the mess but didden do no good. Ain't that always the way? At the

Billy on tap

same time he was razing a stink haff way acrost the world about them Diffidents in yer Serviet Onion, but he cooden do the same thing back home in his own pew.

Carter sure had a big job ahed of him. Sum Americans, mostly Republickins were afrade that they had traded in their Ford fur a Edsel. Like Roseyfelt, Jimmy's big job was gittin' jobs fer lotsa others. Roseyfelt sure dun a good job back in yer dirty thirtys by gettin' yer unemployables in unyforms, callin them the C.C.C. and gittin' them to plant ·· trees all over the place. Them trees cum in handy lessen 10 yeer later, after Purl Harbord, wen them same yung fellas was now in yer Tank Corpse and used to practiss by knockin down all them trees. That's wat they call progress, I gess.

Jimmy and our fella got along like a house a commons afire. Jimmy even ask Pee Air to call him up in yer Ovary Offus once in a wile and let him noe wat he's bin doin' wrong. Pee Air he use to bring his own trubbles to Jimmy wen they was on the fone. Pert neer every weak he'd dile yer Whitehouse on the redfone and say: "Jimmy, lower yer dollar!" Jimmy, he'd jist holler rite back "Pee Air, up yores!"

One big projeck they had between 'em was yer pipeliners comin' down frum yer Blowfurt Sea. A coupla yeers before I thot Jedge Burglar had put the kybo on that after he was giv his commishun, but them reports they make out like that seems to go off with a big bang fer a minit and then gits laid on the shelf with the rest of the best-layed plans in this country. So Pee Air promiss Jimmy that our pipeline wood start cum September, even tho Bergler sed we shood hold in our gas fer anuther ten yeer. I gess Carter got tire of waiting after September, fer he sent out Cyrus in Advance, the fella who tuck over yer Forners Relations frum Hennery Kissassinger, to yer Midleast to cook up more oil.

At that time yer Yank was gittin a lot of his oil from I Ram, and the restfrum yer Shoddy Arabians, yer Abby Dabbyans, and yer Jordanairs, I spose. But nowadaze,

wen Jimmy Carter is back in Plane Jorgeyuh, I'll bet yuh
he's jist tickled pink he saved all his peenuts fer them four
years he was encumbranced in Warshinton, becuz that's
the cheef hope of Amerka fer fewcher oil, is grindin' them
nuts. The Tarzands of ours ain't workin' out too well. And
we may need Jimmy soon fer to keep us in heet. And he
still wants what we got up yer Blowfurt Sea, fer all them
high-nockturne big gas guzzlers drivin' round in his state.
But we better make a deel soon, fer if we hold off Jimmy's
gas too long, he may tern round and cut off our nuts.

Biggest thing Jimmy Carter ever dun in his first yeer in
his offus was to take on them slippry customers, yer oily
cumpnys. He jist rared back and tolled off them refined
distillers that they was a-rippin all of us up the back and
holdin' us over ther barl. Carter sed wat we are tryna find
out up in our country rite now, that them oil tyfoons is
makin more munny out of our allergy crisis than you kin
shake a dipstick at. And the same time as they are rapin' it
in, they are askin' the guvmint fer more consesshuns than
we got in the hole of our township. It was Carter hoo point
out that the cumpnees was gittin fat on oils and we wuz
only gittin' the shaft.

Gay Rites

Can't let 1977 go by without menshun of anuther sepperator, Aneater Tyrant, who dedickate herself this yeer to
seppratin' the men frum the uther boys. I'm talkin' about
yer homeosectionals, and this orange juiced woman start
up a crucifixade agin them among yer Florider citizens but
like all sex acts it spred like wildflowers.

When she first started railing agin yer homo, I thot she
was cricketsizing my milk, and I was gittin reddy to skim
down if she got too close. No, she was talkin' about them
bizzybodys that stick to ther own. Now I don't spose I've
run into morn a haff a duzzen of them kind in all the yeers I
bin on erth, man and boy. Mind you, we git used to sectional preeversion on the farm, fer I've notice yer aminal
ain't too fussy about what he gits with when the heet's on.

Most beests wen they git down to it, is buy-sectionals bilt fer two.

But Anteater Tyrant used the good book fer to prove her point that peeple shun't beleeve in ferrys. She let off a quoat er two frum the Book of Levickedness where it sez that yer averidge three-doller bill type is an abdomination in the site of Jeehoavah and shud be put to his deth. I dunno if Ms. Tyrant red on in that partickler book, but if she did she'd find that not many of us wood excape havin' the blocks put to us. You take Chap 19 where it sez:"Thou shalt not eat any flesh with blood in it." Cansell yer rair stakes. "Thou shalt not round off the hair on your temples or mar the edges of your beard." Bangs is out and don't trim yer beerd. Us farmers gits off even worse:"Thou shalt not let they cattle breed with a different kind." There goes all my hybred hybrids. "Thou shalt not sow thy field with two kinds of seed." There goes my pasture with its alfalfer and Second Timothy.

I know the devvil kin quote scrippature fer his own deeviations but I'm not sayin' this juicer lady wern't sinsear. I git worried about child molestirs of both perswayzions. (Statistickally, them munsters is usually married men with kids of ther own, buy the buy.) I think that's the job of yer pleece fer to snoopervice that kinda goins on, not a ex-bewdy quean hoo is straning her relay-shuns with her Navel producks.

~~Spurts~~ bawl

Biggest thing round our parts this yeer was the comin of Bigleeg ~~Baseball~~ to Tronto. Muntryall was wayahed of us with ther Exposers, and they had beer to boot. But yer blue law always wins over yer brown noser in Trawntuh, so mebby we shood have called our teem yer Labatt's Dry-landers wen compaired up with them Seegrim Hi-landers down to Cuebec.

The wife she thot Bloojay was a silly name, callin' a baseball team after a buncha cornplasterers, but I tole her it was fer the birds that they was named, and she sniffed even more at that, fer to Valeeda, our hed gardner, a bloojay is nothin' but a scavenger, and havin' watched the teem fer the past five yeer I'm declined to agree. And she's all agin speerits in the park, fer the wife and former sweethart's a chartered member of yer WCs to you. Mind you, that won't stop Hawgtowners frum carryin' a brown bag under their entrenchedcoats. How else could they put up with them Aggernuts wat hasn't bin in ther Gay Cups fer thirty yeer?

First game our Bloojays beet the Sox offen them Chicago Whites. Everything looked pritty white that day fer there was yer blizzard goin' on, and I don't mean yer Sockerteem. I don't think anybuddy was lookin fer a cold beer but they mite a settle fer hot wine if yer Bored outa Control had mulled the hole thing over. I wisht the wife had bin with me fer to keep me warm, but she thinks a shortstop is a quick hop to the warshroom. I bin crazy about baseball since I was a member of yer Not Hole club, and we use to come down to Trawntuh in the thirtys to see Ike Boon poppin his flies. The oney ones colder'n the expecktators in the stands was yer Kilty Pipe Band marchin' around with their minny skirts, and playin' "Yer Blueballs of Scotland" like they reely new wat it wuz about.

Teem Canda was at it agin this yeer. Alan's Eaglits was over to Old Vee-enna (I didden reelize Labats stretch that far) fer to revenge the time our boys got run over by Yaketyshev and yer Red Army 11 to 1. They din't have our boy Bobby Ore like they had this yeer. His knee was on the bum, wich sounds to me like a fool of a transplant operayshun.So our boys becum ruffneckers, and if they didden win in ther cups they sure qualify fer yer Lady Bang'em agin the Boreds atrophy.

In the end Bobby was finely give the knee this yeer and hung up his Number Four in yer roof of yer BossedIn Gardings, and I don't need to tell yuh what Parry Sounders thinks of him, he's the best thing ever happen to it. And what about old engine Number Nine, Gord E. Howe. He was still goin strong in '77. Nuthin' Seedy Howe about him, fer he rack up Gole Nummer 1000 this yeer, makin' him one of the Immorals. Oney sour gripes cum out of this celi-bation was Harld Ballhard, the uther con rools over yer Makebeleeve Gardings, wooden let Foster Hooey yer loudspeeker denounce the fack to the Tronto fants, jist becuz it was happenin' out of Harld's leeg.

Rally round the fag, boys

Kulcher

I gess the biggest thing on TV in 1977 was yer Common House Questing Peeriod. Leest it was sposed to be. Every John Q. in yer pubelick was anxious to watch ther own guvmint's affares rite frum the direck end of yer horse insted of 30 second flashes frum yer pressgangs on the nashnul noose. It was all yer idee of yer Grits on accounta they wanted to show off the Merry Charismus of ther leeder and his hie cheekybones. Joe Cluck was startin' to git to be called Joe Hoohoo by this time, on accounta nobudy much except yer Tory party orgynizers had seen him since he got anointed. But ther was roomers Joe was nervuss about leeding with his chin on yer Candied Camera. Ackshully Joe looked a lot better standin' up in yer House than he ever dun walkin' outside it. So much fer facial discrimination.

They soon got rid of all them green blotters on the Common House desks fer it give yer privates member a ghooly glow like he'd bin incarsterated in the pen fer yeers. So they browned them all up with gingbred culler blotter, probly thru a little pancake at them so now they looks like they bin lazin' around yer topical beeches wile the rest of us is stuck at home. Jeens Cretin he still looked a bit green around the gools tho', but that's becuz he had tuck over our fisical affares frum that big clown, Ronald MickDonald, who had quit becuz he disagreed with guvmint policy fer to stop the inflammation. Mickdonald jist sed "Unemploymint isn't working".

Most expansiv kulcher event this yeer was Canda Week, witch is the new name they keep tryna push instedda Dumb Minion Day. Last yeer when the Yank was havin' ther Bisextentacle, I don't think the guvmint give one peece a punk to lite one firecracker on July 1 over the Hill. But Reamy Leveckyou had a ring-tail snorter of a shivaree with his Fate Nation-all on Sinjon's Papeese Day, so this yeer the federasts deesided to go all patererotic with seven daze of celibations, to stir up our own national fate. The

Roamins use to call it bred and circusses wen they dun it in yer Colossalseemen. I don't think it makes the country strong jist to have Canda Week.

The wife she sez the big culchurl eevent of '77 was the pubication of a book won yer Guverning Genrul's prize fer friction, called *Bare*. Now I jist love aminal storrys, I was hopein' all year to git down to Tronto and see that moovy that they maid about a ostridge with a frog in the gullit, yer *Deep Throat*. But wen Valeda tole about this here book by Marryin Angle, my gol, it sounded like yer hardpore cornograffee. *Bare* is about a big brune, but he's about as far frum Whinny Yer Poopoo as yer likely to git. He's one of them jaspers frum the park, a forefoot furcoat and he has a affare with the woman that writ the book. Now, the wife sez this is a mith, fer yer simble minded, but my gol, you take yer averedge bare he don't mith vurry offen with them claws, and if she got involve with that, he musta tore the dickens outa her bedsheets. Kinda makes you wonder if that little Goldielox was all tied up in what they call yer Menagerie-a-trois.

Now I never got to reed this grizzly piece. I'll wate till they make a moovy out of it. They'll probly tone it down fer famly viewing and call it *Gently Ben*. But Valeda she thinks it'd make a ring-tail snorter of a mewsickle fer yer Charlatan's Festeral. I got a good titel if they want it: *On Top of Old Smoky*.

Chapter 7.   1978

Yer Yeer Outa Controls

Do yuz all remember back in '75, wen the guvmint put us under fer yer wagey-pricey controles? A lotta peeple minded that, mostly yer worker wen he found that the guvmint was controllin his wages but doin nothin' fer to keep a lid on his prices, which kept steemin' ther way to the top. Mind you, yer Tories was the first to be suggestiv about all this, but they oney wanted it to be fer a short time. But it was yer Grits put on the controls within the yeer and three yeers later it was the Grits that tuck em off — on accounta they never werk, I spose. But that didden stop the tryin' times we went thru in between. But all that did nuthin fer our yewkanommics. As old Abelinkin sed, yez kin fool a lotta peeple summa the time and summa the peeple alotta the times, but the guvmint goes on makin' a fool of itself alla the time. No wonder sum scientifick this yeer started up a projeck sendin' out raddio sigganals into utter space lookin fer sines of intellygent life. I gess he'd give up lookin fer it down here.

I think it was this yeer that our Infernal Revenoors reel-ize that they wood never cut down on their defickate by jist goin' to the old printin press and terning out a new addi-tion. Sumbuddy figgerd that it was time fer to taper the paper and take the leesh offa our doller and let her float. And she's dun that ever sints — belly up.

But ther's them that sez a cheeper doller is a good thing. We can't compeet with them as is in cheep laber in Kareer, Tie-wan-on and Indyamnesia. A cheeper doller mite get us a yen fer yer Japanee and make us an easier mark frum yer West Germs in yer Common Markup.

Serviets Fallout

Yer Spaced Pogrom got outa controll this yeer too,

wen a Roosian Satelly-ite stopped circumsizing the Erth and cum down in our North-Waste Terror-Torys. Them Servietts was the first to shoot up in the Status Fear, you mind.

Now everybuddy's doin' it, settin off rockits like every day was yer twennyforth a May. Even us Canajuns got one up there. I fergit what she's call — Yewnik or Anus — she was shotup so's yer Innerwit cood be brung into contack with civillyized worlds like *Lavurm on Shurly*, *Starkers in Hutch*, and *Kojex*.

But there's them as thinks that both yer Yank and Yer Red fellas is up there spying on eech other like they dun a few years back with yer U-2-3-4 planes, that used to snap their Brownies as they went booming their way thru yer insomnic wind barrier. Even in 1978 a buncha Roosian cosmicnuts was up there bilding a platform. Sum sed it was plitical platform, uthers thot it mite be a millinery one, fer to house them little spacey crapsules loded with an atomical bum. Or mebby it's fulla little mikeroe-orgasms fer to start yer germin whorefare.

Well, one of them Soyuz beans was bound to split its pod and git out of its orebits, and that's wat happen this year on our own terry firmer. Mind you, yer Yank knew first. Premiere Terdo was havin' breckfust with the boys wen he got this call frum the big Goober in the White House. "Pee Ayuh, has you found yer Satellyite yit?" "No, Jimmy, Justin hasn't got to the bottom of the corn flakes box yet."

I've herd it sed that yer Yanks noo this blame Roosian thing was on the fritz and wern't too long fer outa this world long afore we dun. The week before Jimmy call, Terdo wuz doin' sum Coloradder springs on his skees hard by AssPen, and he took time out fer to visit yer No Rad hindquarters. We have sum of our own fellus down there, wearing their green parkin-meeter eunichfication soots, and I'll betcha they cood have tole Pee Air then. Fer this cood of bin dangerous if north Canda hadn't been so uninhibited. One of them Space drop-outs had hit a heffer the munth before down in Venusasalea, and my gol, yer averidge heffer ain't all that mutch bigger than yer wife and mine.

The most larming thing is if that Serviet satellyite had made jist one more circumcision of yer Erth it wooda cum down upon yer Man Hatin part of New York durin' yer mourning resh hour. Now I don't noe wen they cum to ther sensus last, but it seems to me that the popillation of that big city is about as dense as they cum. There's a lot more inhibitants per square hed than we got up here. And Chicagy and Lost Angleless is even bigger if you takes in all ther outlandish sluburbs.

"Fer ever and ever, Amin"

I know how I'd feel if that loonier modyell cum spreddin' all over Muskokey as fur as Pointa Barrel. We cum offal close to havin' a nukuler catsasstrophy and there wern't nuthin' nobuddy cooda dun about it. Even Barmy Dansum, our Nashnully Offensive minister that yeer, sez

73

now that him and all his brigandears was compleatly mis-
sinform all the time. Reason he didden tell us at the time is
he didden want us to lose any insommonia over it.

The upshat of it all wuz that us Canajuns hadda cleen
up yer Serviet's act, and I don't think we ever got back a
rubble fer our trubbles. Mebby that's why a few weeks
later we swooped down on yer Rossian Embarassy in
Ottawa and root out all them enema agents. There musta
bin a bushy baskit of them northern spys we cot. It wuz the
biggest hall since that typhus clerk, Ignore Goostanko, defecated over to our side in '46, and he has hadda spend the
rest of his life with a paper bag over his hed even wen he
becum a mistry celebrititty on yer "Frontal Page Challis".

yer Clone-in Show

There was one thing wat cum under controll in this
outa controll yeer and that was yer sectional intercorse.
Fergit about Huge Heffer and his Playmates with stables in
ther navals in the *Plowboy* maggazine. 1978 was the year
of yer cell mates. I'm not talking about pros gittin it on with
cons, I'm talkin' about a baby gittin' borned in a testy tube.

Now yer artifishul insinuation has bin around fer quite
sum time. We tride it with our own cattle wen our bull took
a queer tern one winter, but our herferds didden seem to
care fer the bottle stuff as long as they cood still git draft.
But nobuddy had ever tride phoning it in with a yuman
bean. Mebby clonin' it in is closer to it. Fer this was the
yeer they sent in the clones fer to do a man's job. The hole
procremation ring-dang-doo was circumintervented by
havin jist one tiny little peece, a clip of an eerlobe or a snip
of a toe, drop in a testy tube fer to start tiny micro-orgasms
yer eye can't see wen she's naked.

The wife and farmer sweetheart, Valeda, she sez I got
the thing all wrong. She sez it ain't a matter of gittin' yer
Xeroxes off fer to make a baby frum one little cell. She sez
it ain't outa yer famly way at all. The father jist makes a
small depossit in a long thin glass flask, and it gets
transferd to the muther by interjection, same as any old
cow by ~~artyfichul~~ insulation. She's crazy, that woman! I

fish all

74

don't wanna boast, but I never yet seen the testy toob big enuff fer that kinder hankypanky.

It may be hard to conseeve of, but a millyumair down in the States this yeer clum that he had had a carbin copy of hisself made frum sum smallest part of him, then dropped it off to one of them sighentifickal lavatorys and let old Mother Nature take her intercorse by bifurkatin' sevral jillyuntimes. A lotta peeple yelled "Fake!", but this millyumair showed a pitcher of a baby the dedspit of him. Corse we got the same result the ole fashion way, wich sounds a lot more enjoyabull to me. But our boy Orville is the ded clone of his muther, speshully of late years wen he let his hair grow, and looks fer all the world like anuther tired housewife.

Nashnul Yewnitatty

Our biligamal problem got way outta control this yeer with yer Bill One Oh One put up by Reamy Leveckyou down to Cuebeck. Ackshully Roe Bair Boorasser had started this garlickization of langridge with his Bill 222, which frossted all yer Cuebeck angledphones and give them a hedake no bill cood cure. Reamy passed his own movemint in '77, but the rapercussins started early in '78, wen the Sunlife went outa Cuebeck. Reamy had the smoke cummin' out his ears as he accuse them insurer rats of desertin' his stinkin' ship. That was after yer Sun Lifers had called Cuebeck an yewconomick soor, and Reamy sez, well, you know what kinda things run out of a soor.

I thot it was kinda sad fer to have a big cumpny pullin out too soon before they knew the score on yer Repperendum, but the wife sez they've all bin pullin' out too soon down there fer yeers on accounta they don't bleeve in yer berth control.

This was the yeer of Monty Peppin's Flyin Circus, barnstormerin' around the country with John Roebards fer to find out how we were all hangin', together or seppertist. Mind you, Reamy Leveckyou got married this yeer, and he stop using the word separator. I gess the noo wife didden like it so soon after they was into yer holy ackermony. So

75

Reamy started callin' it yer Soverntitty Ass'n, which is a long ways round way of sayin' he was hopin' fer a divorce frum us so's he could live offa the allymoney.

This country is a grate one fer hiring peeples on Commishun fer to publish ther droppins about what's rite er rong about this country, and then putting the hole rang-dang-doo on the shelf and fergittin' about it wen they're all finished up. Sumday they may jist keep a commishun and put the country on the shelf. When Peepin and Roebares finely let off ther report it seem to say we wasn't so wellhung together as you mite like, and nobuddy in Ottawar wanted to heer that. But Premeer Terdo wern't goin' to give nobuddy a chanst fer to exercise ther french-frise this yeer wen he notissed his hed wern't up on top of one of yer Gallup's Poles, so he spent '78 doin' yer Hesi-tayshun Waltz.

The only electionrearing he dun this yeer was throwin' his ball up in the air at yer Tronto Exhibitionist Park wen the BlewJays were starting in season. But a cuppla weeks later sumthing nasty happen wen a littel girlsinger tride to start off the game by singing our Nashnul Antrum bil-ingamally. There was a lotta booin' but I think it was mostly on accounta yer Blooeyjay was making Tronto the place to cum to if yez wanna see a ball game in the worst way.

They bood Premiere Terdo wen he threw his first ball out onto yer pitcher's mound. Everybuddy yell "Yer out!" After that game he was still in, but enny chants of a lection was out. They also boo big John Maybury after he struck out, even tho' he'd alreddy put the old apple over the back fents forty time that yeer. Big John were the oney Jay hoo was reely flyin'. It don't take no branes fer to bray like a jackass. Instedda razzin' at hearin' our Antrum frenched whyn't they all sing twice as loud in Anglish? That was the day Hogtown reely erned its name and changed the cullers of our flag back to red, white and boo.

There was booin' at yer MakeBeleeve Gardings too. I dunno if there was enny during yer Gay Cup down to that Limprick Stayjum in MuntryAll that yeer, but if us Angle-O's wanted to change Bill One-on-One that was sure the place to do it and not by booin neether. That Bill sez you have to speak Garlic down to Cuebeck, so if you wanted sumthin to eet during yer inter-emission you wasn't alloud to say: "Boy, gimme a hot dog"; ya hadda say: "Garkin icky, donny moy yune shee-ann showed avec buckup de moo tard" — jist the way Long John Doofenbeeker wooda sed it. And if we all had dun that I garntee that by the end of that afternoon the entire poppillation of Cuebec wooda bin speeking Anglish outa pure sulf-defents.

yer Roilsplits

If this is the yeer things came apart, the Big Eevent fer the wife in '78 was yer Royl Split atween Princess Marg Rose and Lord Snowjob, better noan as Tony Strong-Arm Jones. The wife she never paid too much mind to terrory-asts and plane jackoffs, but she jist cooden git over yer Royls in the Famly spoilin' a 400-yeer recker of good behaveyer by havin' the first deevorce since Hennery yer V-8. You mind he broke off with Catherine yer Arrogant fer to mary Anne Balloons til he give her the chop. It start up yer Anglecan Church, so ther musta bin Methodist in his madness.

Valeeda figgers royl mirages shood all end up haply everafter like them fairys tails, but my gol, I tell her, royls is peeples the same as everybuddy else, sept they have more of the munny and less of the funny. I've notice that the com-moner you gits, the happier you is. It don't matter if they has all them palaces to go, yer Bucking Ham's, yer Balls Morals, yer Sandwichham and yer Wincer Station. I don't think our Queen has a eezy job, and I don't figger it's enny better bein' second bananner like her sister. As the Good Book sez, neether man nor woman wuz ment to live jist by bein' well-bred aloan.

Midleast Peece

The big noose this yeer was peece in yer MidLeast. That don't inclood most of yer Arbs, yer Shoddies, yer Abby Dabbyers, yer Seeriacks, or yer Key Waiters, but it did bring about a kind of a millstone between yer

IzzRailers and yer Eejippters. Them two had bin at each other's throtes as far back as yer first tennace match in the Bible wen Joseph served in Faro's court.

It was yer present encumbrance in the White House, that big Goober, Jimmy Carter, hoo got them two state-heds, Amour Sedate and Knockyer Begels, together on a mountin in Maryland. The Izzraillies had had nuthin' much to do with them Farodealers sints Moses brung them two tabloids down frum Mount Carmel and tole his peeple the Lord wanted them all to get outta the Peeramid Club. That's wen they all move over to yer land of milky hunny, where they have live ever sints, on and off. Mostly off, I spose, until 1948 wen they move back in and them Pale-steiners moved out and went campin in yer dessert.

But Jimmy Carter was determin to reesolve all this. It had bin tride in the Shineye Dessert by our own Lessly B. Piercin' and he got the No Bell Prize fer his effarts. But by '78 that hole UNO bunch seemed to be about as usefull as teets on a warshtub. So Jimmy invite the two leeders to meet him on nooter ground. I don't know how nooter Jimmy hissel was. He never seem too parshul to that little hard Begel. Mind you, it wern't surprizin Menocker were leery of all them Bed Ones, on accounta they had jumped ther guns on him three time before. They lost all three time too, wich is why yer Izzrailers were in charge of all yer Arb Oh-aces and yer West Banks.

So here was three Goalieths meetin at little Camp David. Sum peeples thot it was High Noon at yer Last Chance Saloon; others sed it was jist a buncha High Holly-days at yer Fat Chance Saloon. But, by swinjer, that little groop bore froot. It was the nite of yer Enemmy Awords it happen (I mean them tellyvishus awords they gives out evry yeer). But rite in the muddle of all these loosers congradu-latin' themselves the show got pre-empteed. In burst Jimmy Carter with a mouthfulla teeth and he usher in Sedate and Begels with "the onvelope pleese," wich contain the real Enemy Awords fer that yeer. I cooda lissen to them two Middle Easterners speek ther peace all nite. Too bad it never becum a weakly serious.

Wimmen as Armed Farces

Speeking of wores and roomers of war, the battle of yer Sexies got a hotting up this yeer. I mind wen I was serviced in yer Royl Muskoky Dismounted Foot at Camp Boredom in 1942 they used to give us sumthin in our porridge fer to make us never mind the girls. It was called yer Salty Peter, and after forty yeer the wife thinks the stuff is finely startin to work. But nowadaze "the girls we left behind" is comin' out from behind and wantin' fer to git in on all the ackshun.

Frinstants, there was this sexteen yeerold girl wantin' to be the first of yer all too few: a fightin pile-it in yer R.C.'s A.F. She had alreddy drived a Unightied Airlions plane with her dad, and she sed it wern't that big a step frum fiddling with yer joystick to oppressing the buttons on a coupla masheeny guns.

Now I know that we had girls in soldyer soots in World War Too, yer CWACK, yer WREM and yer Dubble VD. (Valeda sez that can't be rite, she's positiv.) Mind you, they was pritty well all confined to barracts. But these new ones wants to be in the thick of yer fite, and I kin tell you as a married man and beast and a private member of yer Silent Majorority, them distaffers can mix it up with the best of us. I never seen a woman yet, wen it come to a martial spat, tern out to be one of them unconshus objectors.

And wimmen sure wooden put up with wat happened to men in '67 wen all our soldyers, sailers and airyplane fellers was told to git into the one unyform. I'll betcha if wimmen was pit in chart of our armed farces they wooden stand fer them all to be dressin' the same. They mite even change ther stiles every yeer. Mebby one yeer they'd wear the little tammyshatners over on ear, and kilts with yer spore-on hangin' down, and the next yeer it'd be belly bottom drawers with a bosom's whissle stickin' out of the chess pocket, and one of them bushy beavers frum yer Grenadine Gards on toppa ther heds.

It may jist cum to a pass. In '78 two yung teenyflappers charge yer Defensive Barmy Damnson with artifishul

discrimmynation fer not lettin' them stand on gard fer thee
and me, by yer Infernal Flame in fronta yer Common
House. One old vett in the Leejun Hall in Parrysound sed
we won't see wimmen goin' thru the changes like that in his
lifetime, but I think he's jist wistlin' up his wind. He was in
yer Guvner Genral's Mud Gards (used to be Lord Strath-
coronary's Horse) and I think it won't be long before they'll
all be called yer Coldcream Gards.

Cuminwelth Sports

Good news this yeer was yer Cuminyerwelth Games,
which was the oney time this country hit the Gold Standerd
all year. Fer starters, unlike yer Limprix, everything was
brung in on time and on the munny, too. Oney thing to
worry about was weather that ding-dong daddy frum
Ugandier, Eedy Allmean, was gonna crash the party. He
dint, but peeples cum frum allover yer Umpire-that-was:
Barby Dose, Slinga-pore, Malaise, Gamblya, Gonner,
Grenade-uh, See-Air Lee-Own, Guy-Anus, and even Nude
Ginny.

The games was open by Her Majestic, and Premeer
Terdo cut short his Yerpeen vocation fer to be present.
He'd bin over with his frend Helmet yer Shmit of Germny,
Valerie Discard Disdain of Parisfrance, and Premeer Neel
Sedaka of Japanned. That's the thing he duz best, hob-
blenobbing with furn potent-takes. He's one of our most
successful exporks, and allota peeple thinks he shood stay
out of the country alla the time. He was Morocco-bound
wen he did a bout-face at Games time. He was there fur
yer Queen's openin' whissle.

I dunno wat he talked to our Quean about, but he cum
outa them games babblin' about our constitooshunal. Now
mind, he's blabbed about this before, I think he tuck it in
school and writ an assay on it, and it's stuck with him, and
he's stuck with it like a grammyfone needle. He may not
know how to git ennybody a job or a roof over ther heds,
but changin' the rools we live by seems to be his speshulal-
lity. First thing he wants to change is us sendin' a note to

80

teacher over in Angland fer to let us change our own rools.

Well, Pee Air pert neer got this agreed to in '71 at yer Victorious Confluence out in B.B.C. but Roebear Boracic change his mind as soon as he got home to Cuebec. Seems the French in Cuebeck don't truss that federast Frenchy up to yer Common House. But this summer of '78 he give us a hinky-dinky of what his plans was. Mebby it was sittin' next to yer Queen in that vermin cape give him idees of puttin' the snatch on it and puttin it on his own shoulders.

Meen wiles, the hed of Deef's party, yung Joke Lark, wuz startin' to git parryanoid about sumbuddy tappin' his wire, down at his Eestblocked Offiss: yer offishul chamber-spot of yer Oppositposishun. Joe thot all sines pointed to Terdo, but terned out Pee Air had uther things to worry about on tap.

His wife Mar Grit was bizzy ternin' herself into a moovy actress, nuthin' having develop from the fornogra-phy coarse she tuck in Newyork year before. She made a pitcher on yer French River-Era but she hadda have her Garlic words flubbed in for her cuz she wernt bilingamal enuff. In fack, yer Peepin-Robards report sed that all that Bye-and-Bye Culture and Lingamalism we had had was a 400-millyun-dollar waste a time. Them Anglican saxa-phones in yer sibilant service was sposed to have bin immerse in all that Garlic and they cooden even tell yuh the score after yer Hibitants plaid yer Nordeeks. It look like monolingamalism was in farce rite acrost the country.

Meantimes the Grits wasn't doin too good in yer bile-action bizness. Used to be they'd win 'em all hands down, but in 1978 they lost fifteen rite in a row. When Truedo pass his 59th berfdy it look like the frosting was alreddy off his cake. Sumbuddy had blew it and it look like sumthing new hadda be cooked up. Like the old sayin' sez, we had sold our birthmark for a messy porridge.

One thing wat wasn't cooked was yer books, fer the hole thing was snoopervised by yer Odd-Tory Genrul, hoo overlooked everything the guvmint spent. He brung out his report with a bang. He's a kind of ominous budsman who

"No tappin' up my end"

is sposed to odd-it the guvmint and then kick them in arrears fer 800 pages. Well, this yeer he give the guvmint its wurst report card. The Grits wasn't too happy by the end of this yeer. But I spose it was ther party and they cood cry if they want to.

One nice thing that happen before yer yeer cum to its end was that nice End DP fella from Manytober becuming our Governing Genrul. It was good to have a coupla reel socialites up to ReDo Hall.

Chapter 8.   1979

Yer Yeer with Child

It was Long John Doofenbeeker hoo sed it first. "Canda celibated its Yeer of yer Child by making Joe Clark Prime Minster." Sum say that was jist sour gripes frum a previous encumbrance, but Joe sure made '79 look like a "Leev it to Eeger Beever" yeer with his gangleen walk, tuck-in chin and luvvin' cup eers.

Joe start off this yeer by becumming a world travler. I spose he figgered by goin' frum Hie River to school in Dollhousing in Hallyfacks, and then on to Ottawa, he mite as well go all the way cuz he'd bin everyplace else. So Joe Hoo becum Joe Where?

First stop off was Japanned with Premeer O'Hara. Next was Injure, but that Gandy girl, Indeerer, was out at the time. Where she was in, was jail, wich musta sprised her and showed she wernt as much of a sakered cow as she thot. But she was better off then her fella Packystand premeer, Sofa Car Alley Boot-Toe, hoo had jist bin well-hung fer his panes.

Joe din't spend too long round them Skin-doo parts. He looked at a few chicken and a lotta rocks, but mosely he look fer his baggidge, and I'm not talkin' bout Murine Mactier. He skip Chiner entiredly. It wern't that he didden wanna run into Wackyer Fang or his Number Two, Dung. He jist didden wanna be up agin yer Chinee Wall with Jack Horner, the newest Grit Cabnutminster hoo had terncoated frum yer Torys. Chiner has a quarter of yer world's copulation, but I gess it's still too small a place fer two Elbertans on oppsit sides of the fence. Too bad Joe dint go. Chiner wood have give him a differnt slant on wat makes our own country tick: wheet. As Minster of Trade-in-Commies Big Jack Horner had rung up a full sail of two billyun doller-worth a wheet. I gess them Pekinese was gittin tired of bein' converted to rice.

I think the mane thing Joe lerned was that yer outside world is maid-up of forners hoo can't reed the tags on yer luggridge. Now this wood never have happen to Premeer Terdo. He's too sofisticated fer all that goashery. But ain't he the one embarsed us all by doin' a silly little danse behind yer Queen's back, and slidin' down a London barrister, and made obsoleen jestyers at ye Pressgangs? I dunno which is wurst, a rood fella with too much confidence, or a plite clown fallin' all over hisself. In 1979 us voters was soon to be asked if we wanted to go on bein' led by a confidence man.

Wirld Roolers

But afore that, we was all invested with a countryvershull new Governing Genrull. I was sprized wen the Grits anointed an N.D. Peer fer to Lord it over us all as yer Queens Reppryhensitiv. But there was yer Winnypeg town Shrier all dress up in a plug hat and clawhammer coat, and he nock the spots offa everybuddy wen he made his Speech frum yer Drone in five differnt langridges. Them as had grumble about him not bein uppity Canda enuff fer the job now started to grumble that this ex-C.C.M.'er was now buckin' fer Pope.

Him and his Lily moove into that stately residents, Riddo Hall, and the ole place becum liveleer than it had ever bin thanx to three teenyagers, a muppet of a little boy, and a dog. This was reely the way to celibate yer Yeer with yer Child, by ternin' that stuffy place into a famly show.

Mebby the reeson Premeer Terdo dun this wuz becuz his instinks tole him yer Yeer with Child wood not be too good fer yer groan-up, speshully absoloot roolers. First off this yeer, yer Shaw Palaver got cancle. I don't meen yer George St. Bernard Shah Fester-all down to Nagger-on-the-Lake, I meen that hole Umpire over to Eyeran. Used to be called Purseyuh till them cats went back to yer Muslin name.

Mane reeson yer Muslim riz up agin ther rooler was that they was tired of gittin' Westernized. They didden like

84

ther boots and jeens and wanted to go back to them pointy slippers and yer seven vales. They wanted to take ther shoes off every day at five o clock, tern around and face Decca, listenin' to musick wile they sed ther prares.

Yer Shaw, he had bin prayin' fer yeers to the States, shoutin' "Arms fer the love of Ally" and yer Yank was glad to take his oil without cole cash, and give him lotsa millinery hardware insted. And Palaver din't pay no mind to his peeple wen they started to look revoltin'. He jist sat up to his paliss with his wife, yer Shan, drinkin' cavvyarr, that stuff wich looks like bloobury jam but stinks of fisheyes. Wellsir, it din't take long fer yer Power-that-be to becum yer Power-that-wuz. In no time atall yer revolt hit yer Shaw and yer fit hit yer Shan. They was both boot out in estate of shock by them pointy slippers of yer I-tole-yuh Howmany. Yer Shaw had exiled him, and now it was the vicey of yer versey. And exile fer yer Shaw ment no ile comin' outa them wells fer us.

This ole ock-toed-gin-aryan in the rap-around turdbin was one of the best minds of yer ate senchury. That's why he was called yer I-toleyuh, fer he kep on sayin': "I tole yuh I have seen the past and it works." Well, he sure brung it all back in 1979. Yer oldtime Muslin laws make them two tabloids Moeziz brung down frum Mount Caramel look like Chrismuss presence by cumparson. Our Bible sez "Thou shalt not steel" but if them Muzlins cot yuh doin' that they'd manycure yuh rite up yer elboa. And all that adulterated stuff we tock about, if them fellers found yuh foolin' around extra-martially they'd take yuh out and git stoned —and I don't meen to yer beer parler. Fer one thing, them Moehamids fellas is all W.C.T.U. Drinkin fer them meens yuh becum ther whippin' boy. Mind yuh, they gits into yer Hishash pritty good. Oh, ther not abuv suckin' sum hi-water on yer dubble-bubble pipe. It's Yer O-pee-8 of yer peeple over to them parts. But enny boozin' er foolin' around with adulteruss hanky-stanky and they'll make a rock garden outa yuh. The wife she's a tea-toe-tiller herself and she thinks we cood do with a few of them old Muslin lawyers over here. I tole her to git her rocks off the Cana-

"Kiss me Arfat"

jun way, curling.

Meentimes, on accounta this upheeve-yer-all in yer name of Allah, that elergy crisis broke out agin. Winter of '79 it seemed worsen '73 wen that packidge of Sheeks first got us over a barl. Our own oily cumpnys hadden dun much about the shortedge sints then, sept to put big ads on the TV tellin us: "Us Impeerious Assos is lookin' to yer fewcher." Then they'd tell us about all the munny they had spent dredgin' up our Sink Rudes and drillin' down yer Blowfart See. But it was mostly guvmint munny they was usin', wich is our own munny in yer long runs.

The only quick thing they dun as fur as I seen was to up us with a slurcharge the day after yer Eye-run run out yer Shaw. Now that's fast serviss, uppin us by the quartz, as if we had no ile on hand. But I bin suspishus fer yeers that them oily tyfoons wood use any reeson fer to squeeze us at yer pumps.

Queen amid Shakes

Yer uther Absoloot Rooler in trubble this yeer wuz our own deer Queen, the one over to Angland's green and peasant land. It was sure lookin' green offal erly this spring on accounta all them plastical bags piled up everywhere frum a long garbidge strike. They was hire than yer gards at yer Buckingham's Paliss, so this yeer even a rat cood look at a Queen. But the Quean pack up her orb and septic, and Prints Fillup, and tuck off on a kind of Abby Dabby 2nd hunnymoon amung yer Shoddy Arapeyuns. Fer yer Birdish had got the wind up on yer allergy crisis too, and they wuzn't yet sur yer Norse See wuz gonna throw up enuff.

I wooda thot ther was more Arbs walkin' round PickyerDilly Sirkus that yeer than in yer dessert. They was the oney ones cood afford shoppin' at Harrads, witch was thinkin' of changin' it's name to Harrabs. With all them ile wells derrickin therselves up and down, they had more royaltees than the Queen and yer hole House of Wincer. But I think the Queen was wontin' to git away frum all that trubble and strife stirrup by that uther Anglish absoloot rooler, ther first Prime Mistress Marg Snatcher, hoo was bizzy railin' agin yer railers and yer truckers. Everybuddy was strikin' agin eech uther that yeer in Angland. Even the wives was thinkin' of goin on strike agin ther huzbins and holding off ther conjugular rites, altho' how they figgerd on doin' that and layin' down on the job at the same time, wood put them on the horns of a reel dilemena.

But I didden blame yer Roil cupple fer foldin' ther tense and stealin' away to yer Arbs. I don't think them big Shakes out there had seen a reel big Queen sints that old wise-aker Salmon had his temples bilt, fer to showoff to yer Queena Shebares. Mind you, them Arbs don't have yer Wimmen's Librium, so our Queen probly hadda sit at the back of the tent wen they give her the old sheep's eye. And if yer a gast of honner, yer sposed to swally the blaim thing, pewpill and all. Our Queen is a lady and shooden have to swaller that sort of thing. Mebby she pammed it into her nappykin and give it to the cat.

Spurts

I wuzn't watchin' much hockey after our Bobby Oar got hung up yeer before, but they tell me it was a regler retreet frum Mawscow wen them Red Armed Servietts wipe out yer NH Hellers at the Mad Son Square Gordins, where yer New York Strangers plays with eech others. Alan Eaglesmen, who had deranged this hole serious, was so sore a looser that he folleyed them Reds alla way out to Kenny Dee Airpore shoutin': "Cum back, you Commonests, it's sposed to be three outa five!" I herd that our ghoulie, Gerry Chiefer, was so fed up with hisself that nex day he tride to throw hisself under a slubway trane. He missed.

Mebby this wuz wat dun it, or mebby Canajuns felt more like kids during yer Yeer of yer Child, but his yeer almost everybuddy started playin with therselves outa dores. Skeein' both yer downers and yer crotch country, skatin' both on speed and figgers, toeboggling, shmoe-moebeeling, bog sleddin', everybuddy seem to be out on ther weak ends instedda inside watchin' expectorator sports on the TV with a bag of sillycornchips. Mebby they got tired of watchin' ther home teem blow it on the toob, and they wanted to be outside with ther pores open, blowin' ther own horns fer a change. Anyways, this yeer the hills was alive with the sound of mucus.

Diss Asstirs of 79

Ther was sumthin elts give things a bit of a glow this yeer. A big atomical plant hard by PencilVaney started havin' trubble with its piles. It was call Three Mile Ile, and it was startin' to git a permamint hartbern frum all the hevvy-water bubble-up in its reactionarys. If it hadda gon off as unplanned, it wooda bin a erth-shakin' belch, the kind we dropt off on yer Japanee at Hero-Sheeny and Noggasock-eye. In Wirld War Eleven (II.)

Everybuddy for miles around evvacinated therselves to the sitty of Harseburg and wated fer them mushroom clowds to cook up. All that happen was a few cows had ther udders start to glow in the dark. Funny, I bin drinkin' irraddlyated milk fer yeers and thot it was good fer yuh. They're still havin' trubble down round them parts, and them big nukuler tubs has all shet down and hasn't ope up since.

Now if ther's any place is into them kinds of waters hevvier than yer Ewe Ass, it's us up to Canda. We started makin' our urine-anium up to Chock River yeers ago, and we bin radium-active ever sints. And our Hydra heds (Power to the Peeple) in Ontaryo has been prolifferatin' our nukuler fishin all over the place makin' our provinss a place to stand and a place to glow.

After this Threemile blow-up most of us wern't feelin' too sickure about our own anatomical inhallations, speshully after the nite that little trubble-maker, Docker Morton Skulemarm, the coronary-that-wuz, went down to our Peckering plant and snuck past the commishunair sposed to be on dooty. He walked round the hole rang-dang-doo without nobuddy payin' no mind and left his cal-lin' card on the way out, so's everybuddy wood know he'd bin.

Ther shooda bin maryoldnelly to pay fer this, but it all dide down almost as soon as did them Harseburger cows with the lit tits.

Anuther skeer we had this yeer was the comin' down of yer Skyflab. This big ded-wate of a space lavatory had bin doin' its ore-bit sixteen time a day fer a cuppla yeers and was finely resolving to give up and hed fer home. But sints it had unmanned itself long ago, it didden reely have any partickler idee of wher to go. Insted of Hewstun, Taxes, wher it cum frum, it was gonna land at Random, wherever that is. Anyways, by now it didden know it's NASA from a hole in the ground.

The wife was nerviss it wood cum down on us jist like that Roosian satelly-ite. I tole her she was fulla old wives' tails, and that I persnally was hopin' this big extry-testyal meatierite wood fall on our farm so's I cood charge the summer strangers that cum every yeer a doller fer to look at it. But we have relayshuns in Tronto the wife and I, and one of them is a charitabull accountant hoo knows more about munny than the peeples that has it. He tole Valeda the Infernal Revenyou wooda took mosta that munny fer taxes, on accounta they consider this man-maid space truck to be imported mettle from the Staits.

Yer Skyflab finely cum down in yer Grate Oss-trailyun's dessert. That spaced bunch in yer Hewsome Assterdome sure missed ther calling by a cuppla continence. They figgerd her to hit Newfyland one minit and change ther minds to Afferka jist off yer Injun's Otion the next. Them scientificks ain't such a calkillatin' bunch as you'd think.

Anuther dissasseder wich was perverted frum happenin' this yeer wuz out in a neer-slubblurb of Tronto called Miss-assty-sogass. The wife and I was pratickly eyewitlesses to this partickler exploid, on accounta the moemint it happen we wuz drivin' up yer Queen Lizzybath's Ways, havin' jist cum back frum Nagger Falls, wher we dun a rerun on our hunnymoon, celibating our 25 yeer Sliver Analversry. The wife sez that's a fib. Mostly we jist tocked about our twenny-five yeers of holey ackermony. Valeeda sed if we had tride to reenacked it all, I wooda bin the one hoo ended up cryin' in the bathroom this time.

So we was Parrysoundbound late Sardy nite when this big Roaming candel lit up a sky that had bin as dark till then as yer hipspockit. She musta bloo 300 foot in the mid-dair then damped down and smoked fer ten minits afore she whoosh up agin. We jist went strait home instedda stoppin' to find out wat brung on this partickler holeycost. Nex day we lern that a lotta chloreens had bin blown every witch ways.

Yer good gray Mare down to Miss-assy-saw-gass, Haze All Rapscallion, was on the job minits after the big blow-up and started evvacinatin' a quarter millyun peeple. It wuz the most sucksessful pull-out since them Germin Luststrafers had blissed London in 1941. The Mare showed she had a flare fer this sorta thing, but now we shood all be consern about this secretiv dangeruss gas and kemiculls they bin passin' thru on the rails crost the hole country fer quite sum time. Is the guvmint gonna keep us in the dark til the nex fireball lites up our life? What Canada needs is a Freedom from Inflammation Act.

Federast Leckshun

I spose the other big blowup this yeer was yer federast lection wich was announce jist before April Fool's Day. Fer two yeers the Grits had bin holdin' off goin to ther countrymen and lettin' them exercise ther frenchfries. Yer Gallups poles had got in the way of yer votin' poles, on accounta Terdo wuz the low man on your token pole. But he finely cum on the TV one nite and ast everbuddy fer to give him a man-date. I didden know he was havin' trubble gittin femail compny now that he wuz a swingle dad.

To make things werse for Pee Air, Mar Grit brang out her unexpurgatoried biograffy, *BeYond Treason*. The oney thing she sed bad about her prim minster husbin wuz that wen it cum to spendin' a penny, he was titern the bark on a sickamour. That book probly help him on his stump morn hinder his shampain. I susspeck his two cowhorts, Keeth Daisy and Jimmy Cahoots, got her to publish at this time to see Pee Air wood git a simppithy vote.

But mebby Joe Cluck got more simpathee votes from peeple who had lost ther luggridge by Air Candida. It's hard to figger what makes minds up on yer way to the ballet box. Neether side ever talked about the same issyuhs when they was flappin' ther gums. Terdo kep bleatin' about his Constitootional. I thot he lookd fit as a fidel, but tern out he was tocking about a old peece of paper over in yer Privy in Angland.

Joe Clark spoke up about morgridge paiments and sturd up a lotta interest. It was the first time my eers had purk up at the menshun of throwin' a few bucks in the way of us Homoaners. Sum renters thot it was not fare to them, kinda like robbin St. Peeter's fer to pay off St. Pall's. They needen wurry. Nuthin' ever cum of this tempt to cut down our tackses and put us in a differnt snatch bracket.

The one thing nun of yer candy dates every menshun was the invested littigation of yer R.C.M.P. The guvmint had commishun them MacDonald's peeple fer to do this, figgerin' they deserved a brake, I spose. They sure musta liked bein' treeted, fer they took over three yeer of expanse-account meels fer to find out whether our half-Nelsoneddy Strongarm boys had bin burnin' ther barns behind them and tappin' our wires. I don't think hardly anybuddy in this country gives two hoots in Hull weather or not them Musical Riders has a claws in ther contrack fer to let them bust into peeple's homes, or start sniffin' out ther T-4 Shorts. The oney undercover stuff peeple wanted was Marg Trueso's skinnyannigans. Nobudy wants to pleece our pleecemen.

Jist before the lection they got all the partyleeders on TV fer to argy with eech uther. Weather the lection was decide by any of this is hilee debatabull. Pee Air sneer a lot in his I-scream soot, Joe Clark laff like he was hyperventlatin', and of all three I wooda sed Eds Broadsbent won it hams down. But yer NDippy theemsong was still "Yer Impassable Dreem", so what good did it do him fer to be the Masterdebater?

Cum Joon yer Grit wuz no longer it, and yer Tory wuz in his Glory. But they dint seem to git down to bizness rite away. Fer sum reeson Joe dint open yer Common House till Ocktober.

Once they wuz in, it wuz yer Tory tern to start loosin bilerections. But the day after they had lost one out to Prints Albert (Doofenbeeker had barely time to settle in his grave before he musta rolled in it) and the tuther to yer End Dp's out to Contraception Bay, Jokelark's seet count was hangin' by a thred. But low and beholed, that was the day Premeer Terdo resined hisself! My gol, ther was jist one vote atween the two big partys if yer Broadsbenders went to bed with the Grits like they offen do, and yer Sociable Credit Cards jist staid on the sidelines a grinnin'. Then yer Squeeker of yer House, hoo's a Grit, wood have to brake the tie, and gess witch way he'd jump. So Pee Air resine wen Joe Clark seem to be a shoo out.

Pussyfootin' around Three-Mile IIe

Mind you, it oney last three weeks afore we had the second cumming. But in the meentimes all the Grit hares-a-parents started jumpin outa the woodwork fer to clame the thrown. But yer best-laid men's plans all cum to a knot, wen Bingo John Crosby brung out his Black Chrismuss budgie, tryna up everybuddy at the pumps fer 18 sense a gal. The Grits called him a wanta confidence man and brung down yer House jist like that strongfella in the Bible, Sampson Shears. Ther's sum as sez the hole thing was a Grit plot. Terdo had jist pertend to quit so's he cood git all them standin' ovulashuns from the other side of yer Common House. He probly planned to have all them complimence frum Joe Cluck and Ed Broadband maid into TV cammershuls fer the next eleckshin. How cood they shoot him down on the next stump wen they had alreddy over-prazed him at quittin' time?

Joe Cluck's Yeer of the Child was over. He had finished this addledlessons and now his age of manurity was about to begin.

Chapter 9

Yer Yeer of yer Reeruns

The reeruns is sumthin peeple gits in the summer on TV, but this yeer we all had them strait off. It didden hardly seem no time atall sints the last time our gloryfride leeders had been on yer shampane trale. It look like this yeer's leckshin was conseeve on the nite of yer last one, jist nine month ago. This was all the jestation period it took fer the Grits to be just as far ahed of yer Tory up yer poles as yer vicey had been of yer versey a yeer ago.

The mane differents was in the way the two of them run this time. Look like Joe was tryin' to be Terdo, breethin' fire and gittin off sum snappy wan-liners, and there was Pee Air standin' in the shadders with his toe in the rug hopin' not to be took notiss of. And you wooda swore the TV ads they put on was eech dun by the opposit party!

At the same time, yer States was goin' thru ther primermarys, and even tho they wern't fer anuther nine months, they was alreddy a-whoopin' it up in the bush-docks. It made our fellas look like they wuz standinstill, fer our shampain wuz sure crawlin' along like a consteepated canalhorse. This was deliverit on the part of Yer Grits, run-nin' ther candy date by keepin' him stockstill and not lettin' him ope his mouth about his constitooshinull. It was yer bumponalog teckneek, and by swinjer it worked.

There was a forth party, yer Sociable Credit Cards, but they had perty neer extinkted themselfs after they loss leeder Reel Cowett. But this yeer a fifth party riz up with a few tokin' candied dates. This was yer Ryenossasserass Party, witch look pritty much like yer hippy optimist sept they is more horny in front. Ther leeder was a forty-pound ryenose frum a Cuebeck zoo. His platform was re-enforce concreet and I think alla his candied dates lost ther depos-sets by actin' so silly. In Canada yuh don't git into power by doin' foolish things; nossir, here it seem to werk the uther way round.

I won't hold yez in suspants. Yer Grits was back in like Erl Flin. It wern't sumthin we wuz gonna have to git use to, fer I have spent most of my yeers man and beest under a Grit guvmint in that Common House. We had that King McKinzy on the throan fer 25 conexecutive yeers, so it ain't like we hadden bin inockulated up to it. The wife and former sweetart was glad that at leest it was a majorority guvmint, witch ment nun of them wood be gittin' undercovers in bed with anybuddy elts.

Anuther thing had a big reerun this yeer was gold. In 1980 she was heddin' fer a thousan dollar a ounts. The best deposset I had all yeer was not in the bank but at the back of me mouth, 18 carrots full a fillin. By 1980 I think them Arbs had got fed up with all that paper we was throwin' at 'em fer ther oil. Funny thing was, it still took the same amounta gold fer to buy barls of oil as it dun yer decadents before. The wife thot it mite be nice fer to git back on yer gold standerd, and git offa yer oily standerd, but I still think the reel gold is wheet. Don't meen a thing to have glittereerings if yuh got no fud to put on the table. I think it's time to git back to everybuddy havin' a Vicktery Garding, or it'll be like Germny in yer twentys wen it tuck a weelbarrer fulla money to buy a cuppa cawfy fer breckfust, and two weelbarrers to buy the same cup fer supper. Well, they sure fix that inflammation all rite, with Hitler and his Nazty Party, when he solve our hole Depressyun fer us by dreemin' up World War Too.

Yer Big Boy Cot

One thing wat was sposed to have its reerun this yeer was yer Limpricks. Canajuns was still buyin' tickits on yer Blotto Canda fer to pay off the last one in '76. This'un wuz sposed to be split atween yer Yank and yer Serviet. The Yank part cum off all rite at Lake Plastid, but Mawscow's part got boycocked. The wife thinks it was on accounta yer Serviette teem gittin' beet at the hocky by yer Yanks, but she don't watch the Big Bad News, and I tole her it was all over sum of them Reds marchin' in AfagHandstand.

This is a place hard by Cowbull, north of yer Himmelupanlayuh Mountings and yer Affganz is a wild buncha tri-bull peeples. Wen them Rooskies started hounding yer Affgan, they didden reelize what a whore-nit's nest they wuz into. Up til this time, I jist thot that a Affgan was sumthin the wife laid on the pieanner till she got friggid and tuck it to bed.

Dancin' sheek to chic

Well sir, that shure put the kybo on the secund haffa yer Limpricks. Even tho' yer hed Limpricker Lord Killanolin sed the hole rang-dang-doo was gonna take its place cum Helen Hiewater. Ackshully yer Lake Plastic games cum up a bit short with yer snow. It's too bad we coodna let them Roosians play yer Affagahandstanders in our own Limprick Doomed Granstand. We cooda lent to them Affgans the coach of yer Trontuh Aggernuts, Forestry Gregg, jist afore he went off to yer BenGalls in Sinsinatty. Any

97

feller that got his trainin' with yer GreenBay Packies cood handel a scrimmedge like that.

But the big Goober in the Whitehouse was all fer sankshuns agin them Reds. Jimmy was gittin nowares tryna free yer hostiles in Eye-ran, and he wanted to let everybuddy in on the fack that that hole Serviet parta the world was personal-non-gratin with him. Jimmy's reel fite was with yer Publicans, hoo had bin accewsin' him of bean soft on yer Commonests, so I spose he wanted everybuddy see him git hard in front of us. But these sankshuns weren't gonna be tuff on him, jist his farmers. He figgered on starvin' a few millyun Roosian pheasants wood make them sit up and take notiss. But the best way to hit yer Commonest Blockers was rite in the gold meddles. Don't compeat agin 'em, and take the fixins rite outa ther Limprick Soupybowl. Terns out our athaleets' feats was the oney thing held back frum them Roosians.

Yer Seperendum

This yeer started sumthin that is probly goin to have its reeruns fer yeers to cum if that little Reamy Leveckyou has got sumthin to do with it. Him and his Opposit Posishun, that big Clod Ryan, kep putting out Wipe Papers as a kind of bloosprint of ther idees. Reamy finely named the day long bout April, fer to call the banns on our big deevorce, altho' most peeple calls it a leagle sepperasian.

Wellsir, we'd shure be in step with the resta yer wirld if we all dun the splits. This was the yeer a buncha Castrohatin' Cubists clum over the wall of yer Poovian Embarsy in Havanner and ended up in Floridder. There was a Saskytunafish M.P. name of Dick Collver wanted to change the name of Regina to Collver City, jine up with yer States and change our nashnul antrum frum "God Save Our Maple Leefs" to "My Country, What's It to You?" The new Hollander Queen got in Dutch with sum of yer yunger subjecks and pert neer got stoned on the way to git corryonated. Them gentile Hollanders is the peeple that used to tiptoe thru ther juleps.

Yer *moment criteek* cum fer us in May this yeer. To Wee or not to Wee as they say in yer garlic langridge. Wood it be tales I win, or heads up you? I persnally have always felt that the peeples of this country is inseprabull, so much so that sumtimes it takes the pleece to git us apart. Wen the Eyes and Nose was all counted, it tern out sepperashun wuz a big Nono. A lotta Canajuns breethe a big sly of releef and went back to sleep.

Rite away Premeer Terdo started talkin bout his Constitooshunal agin, witch the Berdish had bin keepin for us over to yer West Minister's Abey. Funny thing, them Berdishers don't have one of them old Privy peeces a paper therselves. They got a Maggoty Charter witch garntees yer Hiddyuss Corpus, but they don't have no Declaration of ther Dependents like yer Yank. And yer Yank gits around his by swallying yer fifth. But Terdo herd roomers that Reamy was plannin' anuther Pop yer Questin time in Cuebeck, so Terdo figgered he shud pastryate our B. and A. Act, soon, so he cood pop the constitooshunal before yer Sepperendum becum yer Neverendum.

Unjust Desert

One thing that won't be reerun is wat happen this yeer over to Eyeran. Worsted freeasco sints yer Bay of Prigs: a buncha helluvacroppers hedded fer downtown Terror-ran to rescue them sostages, but they run into injun trubble and had to dip down into yer dessert. But how was they plannin' to git past all them beedy-eyed Muslins and mittle-ant stoogents gardin' them sostages? Jimmy Carder's laffinstock went up in yer Purrsian markit that day, but it wuz pritty sad fer the yung fellas famlys at home that wanted them to cum back.

There's sum as sez Jimmy wuz desprit fer to make a good show-in aginst Tedsy Kenneyday in yer Democrappic Primer Marys. But I can't bleeve he wood risk the hole wirld fer to save his own seet. The wife thinks this hole Earran sostage sityayshun wood a bin cleered up in a minit if they had let Tedsy Kenney drive yer Shaw home from the hostable.

By swinjer it wernt a munth later wen them Pickadilly Commandadildos frum yer Berdish Army showed us how it was sposed to be dun. They de-holed-out sum Terrorassts inside yer I-run Embarsy over to Londonangland. It was dun quickern yuh cood say wambamthankyewmam. It was jist like in them James Blond moovys, oney these mask marvels is fer reel, not frickshun. They first started all this out in yer Librium dessert in Whirl War Too, nockin' off members of yer Germin Pansy divishuns. Ther ain't no rank patches on them so you can't tell a lancedcorpral frum a frigideer. Why dint we send them fellas into I-run Embarsees all over the world? If we round up enuff of ther diplomats and diplomatresses we cooda dun a trade-off fer all them incarsterated Yanks. Make a fair exchange with yer Burro of Missing Persians.

Domestickle affares

But instead everybuddy was fussin' about ther own selfs, like gittin' a tankfull at leest once a week,speshully after Eyerun and Earack went to war, cuttin' off ther barls to spike ther faces. And speshully after that budge-it brung out in November this yeer witch made everybuddy morn so much that it wuz called yer Nashnul Elegy Polissy. Alien McKickin was new to yer Infernal Revenoo and this was his first budgie but it was a ring tail snorter. Wat he dun that nite was wat them Sassakatchyouwanners had dun by sittin' on ther pot ashes till our Supreems Cork put a injunkshun up them. It's not offen that guvmint nashnulizes sumthing that awreddy works.

Petey Luffhed was jist as mad as them oily tyfoons frum yer Shell, yer Golf and yer Texassco. He clame them Ottawawans dint know ther oilwell frum a hole in the ground, and that was jist wher he pland to leeve it. Even his fella Grits in the Common House wuz scared to stand next to McKickin in the warshroom. They figgered if he seen you had a good thing runnin, he mite tern round and try to nashnulize it.

All this so-call robbin' Peter fer to pay Pee Air started

up a buncha Sepraters in yer West agin. They was called yer West Fed Uppers, and they was morn a little stampeed off. Speshully wen yer Grits went all the way down to Maxyco fer to buy sum oil at whirled prices instedda payin' 75 preecent of the same price in Elberter. And Premeer Terso went all the way to Shoddy Arapeyuh fer to git sum more. Now we don't know fer sure if he pull off a oily deel with yer Grate Shakes. He tuck along his little boy Sashay all dress up in a Ayrab barenoose.

Ther was little Sashay's dad dancin Sheek to Sheek with that Shake Yabooty. He has a little boy of his own, wares the barenoose everyday to skool, and he was hopin' to git him a Micky Mouse outfit. I bet Terdo tride to sell him the CBC.

Jimmied Out

Another ree-run that dint happen this yeer wuz that preevious encumbrance Jimmy Carter. The big Goober went back to bein a Plain Georgian cum November. He got berried in a landslide by that moovy actor, sixty-niner Runny Ragin. (It wern't our Geritol Regan; the wife and I figgerd out they was two differnt fellas, not jist the one puttin' us on and off with a wig.) But them Gallupin' pollsters had sed it wuz gonna be a cliffhungover, figgerin' Runny jist a sliver ahed to git his seat in yer Ovary Offiss. It was sposed to be a tossoff, but it tern into a lamslide.

Do you mind this happnin' before back in '48 wen that Hairy little Trueman was spose to looze and then he tern round and beet the sox offen that fella with the tuthbrush mustash lookt like the groom on yer weddin cake, Dewey Tommy? Now all them Publicans was kickin' up ther victry heels, but yer Demmycraps wuz warning that it cood leed us to the reeruns of DethValley Daze, a old TV serious that Ragin' had bin in charge of before he becum yer M.C. of yer hole States.

Runny Ragin hasn't stop smilin' since he got the part of Precedent. And he's got all kinds of plans fer his nabers on eether side of him, us'n Maxi-Co. He wants us to go shares on our gassin oil and he'll give us back sum hiflyin pollyution by dropping a little acid into our rain.

Lowheed makes oily concesshuns

Yer World's Serious

You'd think I'd be menshunnin' yer Gay Cups this yeer, on accounta it was a change frum yer Exximoze and All-Wets, fer they moove it to yer I Never Winn Stayjum with them Hummilton Pussy Cats. But the lessen sed the better. If they had settle yer Nashnul Allergy Polissy with a feetball game, then all us Easterners wood be freezin in that park.

No, the game that tied the wife to her toobs this yeer was baseball. I don't bleeve Valeda's watched a baseball game sints we used to play out in the fallow pastyer behind the barn and had to quit wen sumbuddy slud into what he thot was third base. But she had red in the papers about this plair, George Brett, hoo wuz the biggest hit-man in the hole of yer bigleegs this yeer. But he got a even bigger pile of attenshun wen he becum the butt of a lotta jokes wen he cooden slide fer home on accounta his hemmeryoids. I dunno wen the problem first pop-up, but I tell yuh I can simfonize with poor George. Ever sints I was 15 yeer old, I got the same thing by reshin' outa a warm bed at six in the mornin and strait onto a cold bicycle seet.

This poor fella cooden even sit a game out; the only part he reely enjoyed was standin up fer yer Nashnul Antrum. His docter was needlin' him to go thru sturgery, but I found the anser, not in my local Rextal drugstore, but in our grannery. Yessirree, it's weet bran, George, nature's broom that makes a sweeping statement but is still gentel in the corners.

A Real Canajun Hero

One yung fella dun it all. 1980 may be noan as Yer Yeer of yer Run, a run witch shood be re-run every yeer in his honner, and nobuddy had more of this than he had.

Terry Fox start out pritty quiet, at the tother end of the country frum witch he came. He dip his artyfishul laig in yer Atlantick off Newfyland, and started his run to the tother end of his country. Funny thing, nobuddy paid him too much mind till he faled at wat he tried to do. Roundin' the north shore of Lake Soopeerier (a lake that cooda bin named after him), he hadda give up his serch fer helth fer everybuddy that had canser like him, and they took him back home. But thaf wuz wen the rest of this country woke up to wat he was tryna do. Crossin' this country has bin dun before by canoe, dogteem, bysickle, and even two feat, but nobuddy ever before Terry Fox had tried it on his last laig.

He was hopin' sumbuddy mite give him a littel munny fer canser research, mebby a hundert thousand doller before he got thru, but I don't think he'd maid that much by the time he grounded to a stop. But wen people reelized wat he was tryna do frum sea to sea, in the middle of the rest of us all squabblin with eech other, they up and razed twenny fore millyun fer canser. It's like the Lord sed: "As ye lose yerself, so shall ye find yerself."

Terry Fox is the kind of peeple you reed about in histry books fame-us fer all time. He was bilt of the same kinda stuff as them explorers that uncovert this country in the first place. But he made this country discover itself at a time wen we wuz all wrangling like ally cats. Nobuddy in this country has ever bin a bigger creddit to the race, and I mean the yuman race, than this young feller hoo put this country back on its feet with only a laig to stand on hisself.

Chapter 10.   1981

Yer Yeer of Yer Disable

There's morn one way of being disable. Terry Fox prooved one of them cood work meerkles. Did you ever watch yer Disable Olimpfix? They got one-laiged hy-jumpers kin go hire than a baskybawler's hed. They got baskybawl plairs in wheelychares cood take on yer Harem Globetrots! And then there's the ones on yer side-lines that looks unco-ordulated but inside ther heds wher yew can't see, they got a mind like a compewker. Our guvmint leeders is the egsact opposit. They looks like regler foke with normul branes, but inside they are mentully disable and they're takin' the hole cunntry in the same direckshun.

Yewconomicks

This wuz the yeer that our guvmint made sure by the end of it that we was all fiscally disable. They handi-crapped us with a bludgit that didden make no cents. It made the assidrain they keep droppin on us seem like a poorfumed sitzbath. Fineass minster Alien McKickican becum the strawboss that broke our Canda's back.

And he never dun it a purpose. I don't think he ever noo wat he was doin'. That's the trubble. He was offal good at yer Forners Affares, but I don't think he noes no more about yewkonomics than I do about playin' golf, and the oney good balls I ever hit wuz one day when I step on the garden rake by misstake.

He was anointed to that job by his boss, Terdo. If McKickin don't knoe nothin' about a doller, then his boss noes even lesson that. Now Marg T. in her book clames Pee-Air is titer with his munny than the cheeks of a heffer in fly-time. But that's becuz it was all give to him erly on, and he's never had to worry about the cost of livin' it up. Wen you got a sunuva millyunair pluss a batchler in charge of yer Fine Antses, look out!

I have never herd sich a catterwall as went up in this country after they brung out that bludgit in November. And we're still kickin' up a fuss about it. This will go down in histry as yer fussbudget. It musta bin plant in yer spring of that yeer, but by the time it cum out in yer late fall, it was awreddy obsolene. This was a boom bludgit, but by the time it got to us, it was bust. The guvment was tryna cool us down wen we was pritty well friggid out awreddy.

The yeer before's budgie was call yer Nashnul Elegy Polishy, and I spose it was a tempt to pour watered munny over trubbled oil. It's no seecrete that we don't own our own country, and I bin sayin' fer yeers it's time we bot ourselves back before the Japaknees moove in and sell us all to the Ayrabs. But it ain't yer Ewe Ass of A that owns us, it's them Maltednashnul corpulations that's got their home all over the world and don't have to saloot no partickler flag up yer pole. They're the reel countrys of this world, Exxyon and Coke Coaler and Eye B.M.

But I think the guvment of this country pick the wrong time fer to start buyin' arselves back. God noes I got no respeck fer them oily compnys. Them fellas is the worst rip-off we've had since yer Eatin Cattle-hog, but even that was oney one page at a time. You take that littel Bulgin' cumpny, Petter-a-feena, (and we did): it cost us foretimes as much as it shooda. There's a roomer that a lotta sock-markitplairs with frends inside Ottawar made a killin' on the deel. If them Cabnut minsters started spendin' our money as if it wuz ther own they'd be a site more carefull with it.

You'd think McKickin mite of lerned a bit frum his first try, but this yeer he brung out a bludgit that maid that 'un seem like a pack of Roleades, on accounta this year's muddle had no releef in site. This fella is deetermin to bring down our inflammation even if he has to have us all intrust-raped fer to do it.

And Geritold Boobooey agrees with him. He's the shrivel serpent in charge of our Guvmint Bank, and he sez that as far as he's conserned (and he sure looksit, I'll give

Prepration VIA shrinks yer rails

him that), this is yer Moemint of Trooth. Valeda looked that up in yer Cyclepeederast, and she sez it's the moemint in the ring wen yer Mattedoor takes out his sored and sticks it in yer bull. Well, us farmers had had enuff of that kinda bull and we don't want them to stick it to us no more.

Trubble is, most peeples finds it possible to live with unemploymint becuz most of them has a job. But ther numbers is gittin lessonless. Guvmint peeple have even less to worry about on accounta ther penshuns is indecksed with yer costa livin, wile the rest of us hoo has no indecks jist gits the finger.

In 1981 more and more peeple was in wat they call yer Direa Straits. Yung cupples tryna fine-ants the doorstop on ther first house, or seenery sittizens tryna choose wich can of dogfood they kin afford on ther fix penshun. Pert neer a hunnert thousand of them bussed or thummed ther way up to the Common House one raney November day two weeks after that Budge-it fell on us. And none of them Common Hosers cum out to meet them!

Don't you reelize this hole mess is all our falt? That's wat Geritold Booey, yer guverning genral of BankCanda, tole us the nex day. It wuz time to lower our expectorations, and the guvmint backs him to his hilt. Hoo do we think we are to plan on ownin' our own homes one day? Watever give us that idee? The guvmint has got plans of ther own fer us, on accounta they has got a defickit this yeer alone bigger'n yer Alberta Herniastage Fund. They are walkin thru' the Shadder of the Valley of Dett, and they plan to git out of it on our backs.

But it's eezier fer them to git a loan than us, and they're doin' it. They're still borryin' every day fer to payoff jist the intrust on the morgridge of this hole country. Mosta our munny in 1981 was spent in proppin up our belly-up doller so's it wooden go blow atey sents. I don't think the monoterry polissy they got is werth the paper munny it's printed on.

Yer Norse Louse

Pullitickly this yeer start off with a snow job. Wen the

108

goin gits tuff, yer tuff gits goin', so Preemyare Terdo tuck off fer forn parts, with his skees under his arms. He start off by visiting yer cheef Osterrich, Canceller Kresge, lives over to Vee-enema. It's the same country wher they maid that moovy Yer *Sound of Muzack*.

Terdo clame he wernt on hollydaze but after he had his pliticle chinnywag with Kresge he tuck off fer yer Alp mountings and that's where he got snowdunder. He hadda stay holed up fer three daze amung yer Mattedhorns, and he got delaid so much he hadda skip his nex visit. Joe Clark lost his lugridge, but on this trip Pee Air lost Algereeria! He spent the rest of his time visitin yer Senile-gals in Afferker and giving out Yemen-Aid.

Wat wuz all this aid in aid of? Well sir, yer Consti-tooshun is not the only big bee in Terdo's bonnit. He's con-serned about yer thurd of yer wirld that ain't so welloff. He divides up yer wirld into yer halves and yer halves-nuts, and he clames the first bunch lives in yer Norse and the tothers lives in yer Souse. I don't unnerstand how he cums up with a thurd world when he's dividin' things into halves.

Lader in the yeer, we had a big Norse-Souse slummit up to Ottawah. We invit sum other stateheds, that Westend Germin, Helmit der Shmit, the Premeer of Japand, Suzey Ukeylaylay, the new Socialite, France's Mittleman, hoo had jist put Valery Disdain into discard, Prime Mistress Marg Snatcher, yer Ironed Lady, Master of Cerrymonial Runny Ragin, pluss hooever seem to be Premeer of Ittly that day. Nuthin much cum of it all. Marg and Runny was more intrusted in East-West relayshuns with yer Serviet Onion. Ther intrust was mostly in not having them, and they felt like incloodin' out Japann too, on accounta ther Toyoto cars had give U.S. a coronary this yeer. Precedent Runny was thinkin' of askin' Honda to make the parts grow absent. I think them Yanks had had enuff of any North-South stuff morn a hunderd yeer ago wen they had that not-so-Sibble War.

I dunno wat was said at these seeminars. All them dis-gustin' groops they had was held by yer privates, that's the way them big muckymucks runs ther dipplematick bisness. But nun of them other heds ever seems to talk about yer North-South no more. Sept Premeer Terdo. He's still crazy bout poor peeple all over the wirld as long as ther not Canajun.

Parlmint dissolv itself erly this summer and took off fer a three munth reesess. (It use to be oney fifteen minit wen I went to school.) But this summer they jist seemed to throw up everything incloodin' ther hands. All them Empees clame they cooden git a Oily agreement with that Leech hoo was workin fer Luffhed, and they cooden fix yer forty-seven-day-ole posty strike wich was bankrupturing a lotta small biznessmen and makin ther bizness smaller than ever.

Off yer Rails

The oney Cabnutter hoo staid behind to work things out fer hisself was Jon-Look Peepin. He wuz the one had crosst the country with Big John Roebards so's they cood let off a report about our Nashnul Unititty. Wen they was dun, the Grits was so mad at wat had bin found out, that they shuv the hole thing on the shelf, and put Roebards out to pastyer, and put Peepin into Transports fer to keep him quiet.

Well this Peepin sure made a lotta noise this yeer. As soon as everybuddy had gonn he started cuttin' up our VEEYUH rails, and chokin' off our Nashnul Steam. Now before this, he was giv a guvmint report that tole him not to do sich a thing. I gess Jon-Look was jist doin' to sumbuddy elts's report wat they had awreddy dun to his.

Mosta them ralecuts was out West and in yer Marmtides. The line between Peppy's own home town of Drummervill and his worktown of Ottawa wernt touched. Any lines that went thru a big buncha Libreeal votes wuz dew to git bump up, not bump off. But fer the resta the country, it wuz cold cuts. Pritty soon they'll be cuttin' out sich frills as conduckters. Probly have the kid that sells sangridges run up and down the iles stampin' "This Side Up" on the passinjers foreheds.

The leeder of yer Opposit Posishun had a tuff yeer in 1981. They had a Hark, hark the Clark meetin' in sum Ottawar Creamertorium fer to sharpen up ther shivs fer anuther leedership dissenshun. Joe's chin wuz on the line, and one Tory in three was out fer to shave him offa yer roster fer the nex eleckshun.

Nobuddy much luv yer Grits eether and this wuz proove in Cuebeck this yeer wen that big Clod Ryan got thump on the stump by little Reamy Leveckyou. But yer Tory lost ther last tow-holed, too, when Rocky La Sal pert neer blew his deposset on yer Onion National party.

I got a grate idee. Why not switch the britching on both leeders of yer two mane nashnul partys? Yer Tory can't git hisself unrested in Cuebeck. Yer Grits is in the same way west of Thumper Bay, with even Lord Axworthy livin up to his name after that row with the Statues of Wimmen. So drop Joe Clark frum yer Tory and make him Grithed. He'll git Libreeal votes all over yer West. Dump Pee Air Terso frum his moorings and make him the gratest Tory ever sold. Then yer Retrogressive Preservativs will finely attane ther majorority in Cuebeck. Any change cood only be for the bettors. As the old sayin' sez, shift or git off the spot.

Nantey and Runny

Speekin' of goin' thru the changes, Yer Ewe Ass got a new Present Encumbrance inhogurated into yer Whitehose in 1981 and the hole ringtale snorter of a ring-dang-doo cost upperds of ten millyun doller jist to install this moovy star-that-wuz. Haffa Hollowood was there, more stars than you kin shake a flag at, incloodin' old Blooface hisself, Frank "Mafiasco" Sonata, fer to sing his noo nashnul antrum, "O Say Kin You See, I'm the Don Mooving Rite."

But the best thing of all happen that day was over to I-Run wen them Yank Sostages finely got outa the clutch of yer Cockamaimy Itoleyuh. They had bin tide up in red taip fer fourteen munth, tryna to git that old mulluh offa his assent. But the yaller ribbings cum out this day wen they cum offa the plane and put ther foot on Algereerian terracotta at the same time Precedent and Nantsy Ragin was holdin' ther Inoggerul balls.

In Febyouairy them Ragins visited up our way to Ottawar and ther was a lotta peeple to greet them, mostly pertesters about El Salivador, nukuler reactivists, and sum other revoltin' peeple. Runny, he jist laff the hole thing off, and sed all them placards sayin' "Wore Munger" and "Assid Dripper" remind him of Warshinton. It seem to bother Premeer Terdo a lot more. It's a long time sints Pee Air has bin keen on Partpissatory Demockercy.

Ther was a lot more pertesters around by the end of this yeer. Over to Yerp wher the forners live, haff a millyun yung peeples was on the march aginst croozy missyiles and nooter-on bomms. That's sumthin' that Ragin wants us to have up in Canda. Them bomms don't sound vurry nooter to me, but Ronny clames they is a new improoved deterrent that wipes all the peeple cleen off the map, but leaves the reel estate still standin unharmed. I don't think we need that kinda help up in Canda. Our guvmint does the same thing to us with twenny five purrsent morgridges.

Yer Spay Shuffle

You'd think them Yanks wooda bin leary of shuvvin' more things strait up yer Statusfear after the big cumdown of that Spaceflab. But this yeer they started wat they hope is gonna be a regler shuffle serviss. This time the Astridnuts on bored don't have to go out of ther oarbits, but jist keep circumcising round with eech other till they git the bugs out of a big Spacey bus. This one has lotsa room inside fer yer car-goes, no more liddle space crapsules or spooknuts, musta cost them Nassers a arm and a laig. Well, a laig anyways. It was our country given them the arm, a big long fortyfooter, wen you wooden think we had enuff to rub together to give them the finger.

This first busstrip was jist to sprinkle about sum Satel-lytes all acrost yer Spiro's Nebulous fer to give us more TV Chanels than we kin shake a changer at. But I heer roo-mers about millinery hardwear, like atomical bums. It makes you wunder if the Roosians wood git a lode on with sich things if they ever gits one of these ominousbusses. Mebby we better cleer the air first with anuther dose of yer Salts Talks.

Ther was sumthin' else wich cum to roost over our heds this yeer and that was yer Urine-for-mal-you-hide Fome. This is sum kinda insolence the guvmint tole us to go stuff our homes with. Terns out it brings you nuthin' but greef, dizzyspells, hart palpytayshuns and cansir. A lotta peeple got to be fome-in at the mouth over this insolence, on accounta yer Departly Mental Welth and Hellfire wanted us to pay fer the ripoff ourself wen they had to unstuff ther houses. The guvmint advize peeple hoo cooden afford to do it to leeve their winders open fer to git rid of the poor fumes. In the middla winter? The hole idee of this artifushul insolation in the first place was to seel up our homes with fomes so we cood be in heet the hole time.

Nex time our guvmint is suggestive enuff to tell me to stuff my house with stuff that ain't bin properly tested, I'm gonna git properly testy myself, and tell *them* to go stuff it.

Spurts

Teem Canda got 'em all together this yeer, all the best plairs of yer NH Hellers, incloodin' young Wanie Grezet-sky hoo had bin Oilin' up Edmington pert neer single-hand. And they dun smashin' good agin yer Roosian this time, up till yer finals game. Jist to keep the reckerd fer the past nine yeer strait, they lost, but both sides plaid so good the oney peeple that lost was the crowds that didden cum, and they staid away in drooves if ther was nun of ther lokel boys on Teemcanda. Here we are tryna git a constitootion wen we arnt sure we got a country to cheer fer.

Royl Hitch

In a yeer fulla postie strikes and oil squawbulls, and them Bertish reedin' the riots acts to each other with skin-nyheds overterning London boobys in ther Black Pariahs, it was nice to have sumthin nice happen like the Chuck'n Di show. This was a yeer wen yer Yank precedent and yer Pope got neer assastinated and everybuddy held ther breth

WaneGretzzy makes it big

durin these royl nuppachills, fer they had not-so-civvil underarrest the nite before down to Liverpond. But everything went murry as a margebell under Pall's Bigdome, and it give us the best TV show I ever seen. Sorta *All in yer Family* with crowns.

Yer bride-a-bee, Dianner the Sweets, wuz the hit of the show, and that's no disreespeck to yer Prints of Wails. Mind you, she is haff-royaltease herself, bein' out of the stable of anuther Charles, the Second one, hoo started her line out of Nellygwin, a girl hoose oranges he tuck fantsy to in Dreary Lane. I was thinkin of sendin' the roiled cupple a box of Sunkisters but the wife sez it wernt royl enuff fer them, so we sent 'em off a set of engrave Canajun silver — three shiny new dimes.

They give 'em a shivaree outside of yer Bucking Ham Paliss, and I don't noe wether it was yer Pump under the Sircumtance or jist two nice yung peeple gittin' knotted in holy acrimony that dun the trick but the hole wirld seem to cam down fer a day and wish 'em well, incloodin' even them punkyrockers and skinnyheds that had bin arson around the nite before. Them London pleece, jist two or three of 'em, had no trubble leedin' pert neer a millyun peeple three mile acrost Lundun frum yer Bloodsgate Hill to yer Palled Mall and up to yer Grenadine gards at the gaits of yer Paliss.

Mebby the hole world needed a hollyday frum itself. You hadda have a day like that fer to make a yeer like 1981 worsewile.

Who's
Bossy,
now!

Chapter 11.   1982

Yer Yeer of Yer Unable

This wuz the yeer our guvmint finely admit it didden noe wher it was goin or wat it was doin. Oh, not rite out loud so's yuh cood hear them, but they kep droppin suttle hints. Like Alien McKickin takin his bludgit in fer repares two or three times. He's still tinkerin' with her. He may go down in histry as the biggest tinker this country's ever had.

Then ther was Marg Lalond, yer Minster with All the Energy fer to Mind our Resorces. His hole Nashnul Allergy Polissy was base on the fack that there was a wirld oily shortedge. But this yeer yer shortedge tern into a glut. The glut sounds like sumthing kin happen only to a horse, somers between yer glanders and yer gleet. But, insted, it's havin' too much of a good thing. I never thot it wood have bin possibull to have too much oil around. And you'd think all this wood be the best noose we had since them Opeckers first got us over a barl in '73.

But nosiree, not in Canda it ain't so good. Our oil typhoons started to squawk rite off. And they all started pullin' outa our oily sandpits in case they mite lose a little munny. Oh, they wooden lose ther home or ther farm like the resta us, but they'd mebby have to stint on ther second RollyerRoice or MercyBenz.

Even them Shakes over to Shoddy Arapeyuh was feelin' like they was no grate Shakes. Nowadaze they're all lined up outside ther frendly Household Fine-Ants fer to make a deel with the big Loan Arranger. Now you'd think all them Arbs hadda do was put the plug back in and whomp up anuther shortedge. But terns out all them cartellers got differnt plans. Yer Eyerunners and yer Earakkers is at war with each other, and they'll sell to yer lowest bidder, fer they needs that oil munny fer to keep blowin' eech other part. Yer Shoddy Arbs is in a bit of a blind, fer they owns

Irak sends our Malibooboo back

as much of us as we do, and if they lowers the bum on us, they'll be doin it to therselfs.

And did you think all this gluttage was gonna lower us at the pumps? You must beleeve in the Oil Fairy! Them Elbertans is the one reely takin' it in the neck this time, fer our guvmint is still subsiddyizing forn oil, and makin' us pay more for it than our own, and that's yer hard crude facks.

That's one of the reesons yer Tory party went on strike this yeer, and that strike started all the bells a-ringing in the Common House like they wood never stop. Seems the Grits tried to bring in a ominuss bill about our Oil pogrom. They was tryna pass about a dozen differnt movemints in the one Act, but they got cot in it. Sounds like the old Shell game to me, and that's wat yer Torys thot too. So they started up yer Gong show till the Guvmint thot they was facin' a buncha dingalings hoo'd never let up.

They all went out to their ride-ins on ther weakend and ast the voters what they thot. Two out of three agreed with yer Tory that yer Grits was tryna commit merger on the first decree. I dunno hoo got the No Bell peece prize but the ringin' in our eers finely cum to a stop after about a fartnite. So the call went out fer them Libreals to brake it up, meanin' ther Oily bill, and the Torys also wanted to turn yer Common House into a Reform school. They feel that Parlmint has too many eroded zones fer to be defective anymore, and the new Constitooshunal ain't gonna help anybuddy 'cept all the lawyers that get pade to figger it out.

I dunno wether Premier Terdo is tryna set his lawyer frends up fer life, but the mane idee of his constitootion seems to be to take all the bizness away from Parlmint and put it into the corts. If you got a beef agin the guvmint you kin beef all you want, but you'll have to do it in cort, with a lawyer standin' by fer to transalate all them whereasses and howsumevers-notwithstanding-moreover-theretos into plane Canajun Inglish at a hundert bucks an hour.

I think that all Pee Air has ever dun fer us sints 1968 is make life cost more at our expanse. You take that Metrical sistern. You take it, I don't want it, but I have to, on accounts this yeer it becums ill-eagle if you don't. The guvmint still wants their pound aflesh but everything is now in yer killer grams. Mind you, us farmers told them a coupla yeers ago that we wooden put up with mezzuring our feelds in hectors. We made them git the hectors offa our land, and they've still got us by the akers. But from now on mezzuring in sentupeeds is gonna be repulsory.

The mane reezin our leeders is so dern anxshuss to have leeters stedda galleons is so we won't reelize wat they're chargin us at the pumps. We kicked yer Tory outa power in '79 wen John Crosby tride to up us 18 cents a gal fer our gas, and we bin payin' thru the Grits fer it ever sints. I think yer guvmint figgered them oily tyfoons is too tuff to fite, so they jist jined up with them agin us. That's wat all this metricscam is about, if you ast me. Oney ones ain't complainin' bout it is yer yungfokes. My boy Orville tells me his frends has bin buyin' stuff by the kilo fer yeers.

Crime Pays

They used to tell us crime didden pay. Mind you, as a farmer, I allus knew the crimminul's hours wuz better. But

this yeer the pleece admit they wuz unable to nail a mer-
deruss child molester until they hired him to finger hisself.
You got more chants of winning a hundert thousand dollers
these days by committing mayhemp than by takin a chanst
on a lottaree. This country is in a pritty bad way wen it has
to bribe a killer to show you his grizzly work. Why don't
they make crime leagle and then tax the dickens out of it?
If they dun to them public enemas wat they're doin' to the
rest of us, crime wood be outa bizness in no time.

Big bizzniss

Even yer privates sexters was goofin' up this yeer. The
sail of all them Shevverlays to Earach was a unmedicated
disasster. Thirteen thou of them got ship off to Bagsdad
and seems that every blame one of them turn out to be
shiftless. So the next thirteen thou is still sitting in yer
Hellfacts docs, and the nex twenny thou ain't never gonna
git off the paper it was order on. The hole mess is wat you
mite call a big Malibooboo.

The oney way yer Genrull Motors is gonna git any
munny back is by tryna cash in on the insurgence they tuck
out with the guvmint bunch that deranged the deel in the
first place. But the insurgence don't cover a car that don't
work. It's jist in case God puts on an Act like a war or a
riot, sum kind of nacheral catsasstrophy. But sumbuddy
musta giv them Shevs the Shiv before shippin', and about
the oney thing Gee Em kin do is git down on ther knees,
facing Meccano, put ther hands together, and pray the
Lord to fergive them ther transmissions. I sumtimes think
automobeel cumpnys now adaze needs wat the wife has
always had: Total Recall.

Speeking of turrible misteaks, your Mobile Oil
Cumpny faced a big tragidee when that oil disable rig
went down in a storm off Newfaland. Lord knows them
peeples has had ther share of trubbles in the waters, but
this 'un seemed extry hard to take. And harder still is figgerin' out wat went rong, but I'm wondrin' wether we ain't jist
a bit too anxshuss to git down to bedrocks with our oil,

without worryin' about the lives on bord first. This rig had a safetee sertificut that was outa date by two munth. You wooden git far if you tride to drive a unlicense car like that. Oil, not peeple, is wat you pore into trubbled water.

Kulcher

Tellyvishun got rated so low down that sum peeple thinks that if we want to git better stuff, we'll have to pay fer it. I sure wooden pay fer the stuff I gits to see free. I'd jist as soon lissen to the raydio fer what I need: noose and livestock markit reports, but the slotterhouse reports on the TV is all about peeples.

Most of us is on the Pay-TV now, doalin' out five bucks a munth fer to git cable-ized. They say in a cuppla yeers we'll have more English Channels than we kin shake a stick at. I'm startin to swing my stick at what they're showin me now. Skinflickers is the fewcher of TV some say. If that happens I'll jist git a bigger screen. I'll make it outa 3-ply balsy wood and shuv it rite in front of the TV set.

Spurtsbiz

This yeer belongs to a twenny-yeer-old malted-millyunair name of Wane Gressky. I think it was Leo Duh Roach of yer Booklin Bumdodgers hoo sed that nice guys finish up last. Well, mebby this young lad is the contra-cepshun that prooves his rool, fer he's staid as nice as he kin be. Seems the oney way fer yer underpriledge to be rich these days is thru yer athaleets' feets. In Yankyland sum duz it as moovy stars, and in Maxico yer poor little peeons trys to be bullfitters. But Canda has oney one root, short of yer Blottery Canda, and that's goin' strait to NHL.

Spurts seems to be the oney big bizness that's growing gross as a nashnul produck. Yer Genrull Moter and yer Ford is havin it tuff, Massey Fergoosin may git fingered, but lotsa peeple is willin' to fergit ther trubbles by watchin' two teems whang the dickins outa eech other with sticks. If I was a yung lad I'd be tryin' my darnedest to git on one of them miner midgie teems hopin' sum good ole Scout wood clap eyes on me. I mind the hours I spent as a boy in the barnyard with a curvy stick and a frozen horseball. All I got fer my panes was a life sentence on a manoor pile.

Salty Tock

This yeer seem to be gittin' back to the time wen yer Yank and Yer Roosian started playin' atomical games with us. We've noan that both of them cood blow us all to Kingdom Cum, but this yeer seem to be the closest we cum sints that Roossian Nicky Crushoff tride to sneek sum missey-iles in amung them Cubists, oney 90 mile frum yer Florider maneland. It was Hi Noon ther fer a day er two. And now with them two umpteenagers, Ronny Ragin and Lionkneed Brushoff, we seem to be goin' thru the blinksmanship bit agin.

They're still talkin' pritty salty to one another at them Salty Talks. But peeple are startin' to say this is our Last Chants Saloon to be disarming to each other. There's two kinds of peeples in this world, yer optometrists and yer pessaryists. Yer optometrist sez that this here is the best world that's possible. Me, I'm a pessaryist. I'm jist afraid that them optometrists is right.

One fur the Books

One thing that's happen in the last decadent is that Prim Minster Terdo's Hit Prade has becum a Hate Prade. Ain't nobuddy I kno has a good word fer our Premiere that ten yeer ago wuz up there with yer Beetle and Robber Redfur in yer poppolarity poles. Why? All he ever wanted was fer to keep this nayshun together, and giv them a chants to speek two langridges. That's why he dun his darndest fer pastry-ate our Constitooshunal. The place wat used to have two langridges, Cuebeck, now has passed a movemint so's you can only have sines up in Garlic. The resta Canda never did pay much mind to the Frenchfones in their midst. Funny thing is it's Elberta wher everybuddy is lining up fer corses to speak the Garlic in scools. Sure be ironickle if the West becum yer bilimgamal part of Canda jist wen sum of them seem reddy to fly the coop.

But I don't think it's bein' frenched down the deep

throte that bothers peeples so much any more. And they don't care all that much about Terdo's ramming us with his consitootional. It's the fack that he don't seem to care about much elts in this country that sticks in most peeples crotch. He don't seem to have no enemapathy fer peeples that is homeless. He probly thinks the Housing Crysis is jist sumthing dremt up by a buncha earasponsabull jippsies without so much as a roof over ther heads. He treats us like we're all drones and he's yer Queen Bee. He is the Maree Toilette of Canda, oney he don't say "Let 'em eat coke" wen he talks to strikers.

Canajuns await the next budgit

The reeson he ignore wat was goin' on in this country was becuz he wanted us to be aloan on our own, without no help frum Angland. So Terdo thinks havin' a constitootion is the most important thing ther is. Well, Edie Ameen had one, Chilly has got one, yer Serviette Roosians has too.

A lot a good it duz ther sittizens. But Pee Air was determin we was gonna git this peesa paper and now we got it. I dunno wat good it's gonna do our aboriginal sittizens, or the haff of our popillation we call wimmen. And he sure has cut off fer all time his own provinss of Cuebeck by dee-lin' Reamy out in the middle of the nite, and not tellin' him the rest of them pervinshuls was meetin' in the kitchen over Chinese Food.

But Pee Air thinks the Constitootion is wat gits him into the histry books. He shood think agin. Richer Nixon had the same idee. All Tricky Dick ever cared about was how Histry wood rite about wat he dun. It didden tern out the way he had planned. I think that after all this Consti-tooshunull noncents, Canajans are goin' to tell Pee Air to take a walk—and the longer the better.

Eppylog

In 1972 I was wurried about yer Cuebec Sepperators. I thot if they left it was yer end of Canda. In 1982 there are Sepperators frum see to see, frum Sin Johns to Victororia. The one thing that keeps this country together, is that everybuddy in it lives for and luvs to hate the same thing: watever is goin on in Ottawar. Makes a change frum Tronto, ennyways.

But nowadaze there are uther things to wurry about. Assid rane drops on us frum abuv, wile sumbuddy elts is puttin' died-oxen into our water. The wife and former sweetart is so scared of cansir, she won't fone long distants after six o'clock on accounta the niterates. Nobuddy talks about recessyun no more. They're all worreed insted about a deep depressyun like we had after that panick in the thirtys. Recessyun is wen the fella nex door loses his job, depressyun is wen you lose yer job, and panick is wen yer wife loses her job.

Back in yer durty thirtys, wen the only smut around was on the wheet, nun of us had enny munny and we hadda deepend on the fedral guvmint fer releef. Nowadaze them federasts got no munny and is doin ther damdist to grab wat little we got.

But the biggest wurry of all is startin' to mushroom up agin. Peece in our time is turnin into blowin' to peeces in our time. Is there lite up the end of our funnel? Don't let me put yez under a cloud, but the Stuporpowers is startin' to talk about nukuler warnin' shots, "first strike and yer out," and radient survivors. I gess that's wat passes for hope theze daze.

Persnally I got more fathe in the common sense of common peeples to git together and holler at them leeders fer to save ther skins. If it don't work out, tho', there's a part at the end of yer Bible called the Apocketclips. Look it up at the vurry end of yer Book a Revelasians fer to find out what happens. It's a revelasian all rite. And be sure to cross yer fingers wen you look up yer own end.

When the goin' gits tuff, the tuff gits goin' — Yer place or mine?"

125

Inn Decks